UNWIN HYMAN S[...]

SWEET

SOUR

Gillian
Meldrum

**INCLUDING
FOLLOW ON
ACTIVITIES**

EDITED BY GERVASE PHINN

Unwin Hyman Short Stories
Openings edited by Roy Blatchford
Round Two edited by Roy Blatchford
School's OK edited by Josie Karavasíl and Roy Blatchford
Stepping Out edited by Jane Leggett
That'll Be The Day edited by Roy Blatchford
Pigs is Pigs edited by Trevor Millum
Dreams and Resolutions edited by Roy Blatchford
It's Now Or Never edited by June Leggett and Roy Blatchford

Unwin Hyman Collections
Free As I Know edited by Beverley Naidoo
Solid Ground edited by Jane Leggett and Sue Libovitch
In Our Image edited by Andrew Goodwyn

Unwin Hyman Plays
Stage Write edited by Gervase Phinn

First published in 1986 by Bell & Hyman
Published in 1991 by Collins Educational
77–85 Fulham Palace Road
Hammersmith
London W6 8JB

Selection and notes © Gervaise Phinn 1986
The copyright of each story remains the property of the author

British Library Cataloguing in Publication Data

Unwin Hyman short stories: Sweet and Sour
  1.Short stories, English   2.English fiction —
  20th century
  I. Phinn, Gervase
  823'.01'08 [FS]   PR1309.S5

ISBN 0 00 322260 8
Series cover design by Iain Lanyon
Cover illustration by Chris Burke

Typeset by Typecast Limited, Tonbridge
Printed and bound in Great Britain by Billing & Sons Ltd, Worcester

Contents

Introduction

For as long as there have been people gathered around the fire exchanging gossip, relating anecdotes and telling and re-telling tales of adventure, there have been short stories — infinitely varied in subjects and ideas and situations. There are sad, strange, horrible, humorous, tender, macabre, frightening and romantic stories, from different cultures, in varying styles, of contrasting moods. This anthology reflects the diversity and perhaps, like the tales of old, these stories are best enjoyed read aloud and shared with others.

Opening the collection is 'No Witchcraft for Sale', a thought-provoking, finely-written account of cultural tensions which should offer young readers the opportunity to enter into the kind of discussion which moves from the text into aspects of their own experience. Mike Haywood in 'The Rose Garden' describes an ordinary man in a realistic situation — not an exciting or unusual story but one which has immediate appeal in its warmth and vivid detail. Another sensitive and skilfully constructed story about ordinary people is 'The Goat and the Stars' which explores a young boy's disappointment. In the stories 'Desirée's Baby' and 'Salt on a Snake's Tail' the themes of intolerance and injustice are explored.

In 'The Landlady' we have a deliciously unnerving tale, bizarre and frightening at one point, amusing at the next and with the macabre twist at the end so typical of Roald Dahl. This story might be compared with 'The Pond', another chilling tale which builds up to a horrific and ironic conclusion. In the fast-moving and highly original story by Richard Connell, 'The Most Dangerous Game', we learn much about the storyteller's skill in creating a plot full of incident and suspense and in developing atmosphere and character.

'Vendetta' is a disturbing story of violence and revenge and it is likely that young readers will be provoked into animated discussion about the actions of the central character. In strong contrast, 'The Ransom of Red Chief' is an immediately enjoyable account which develops through a series of highly amusing incidents. 'The Birthday Present' is a sometimes funny, sometimes moving narrative about a young boy's brush with the supernatural. After reading Robert Westall's 'The Vacancy' we are haunted by the sinister characters and the ingenious plot.

Each story in the collection has its own special quality: one is entertaining, while another uncompromising and challenging; one is lively and amusing, while another is deeply disturbing and thought-provoking. *All* the short stories should inspire readers to consider and reflect on the various themes and should act as springboards for students' own creative writing. Three of the writers included here — Marjorie Darke, Farrukh Dhondy and Robert Westall — have contributed personal essays, which students should find especially helpful in understanding and appreciating their stories.

The 'Follow On' activities at the end of the anthology offer ideas for discussion, for writing and for further reading. They are particularly designed to meet the needs of the General Certificate of Secondary Education and to encourage students to respond to the short stories in a wide variety of ways: through full class and small group discussion and through a range of writing assignments. They also offer a range of approaches for English and English Literature which will help students of all abilities, whether in building up a coursework folder on in preparing for essays written under examination conditions.

The suggestions for assignments are structured as follows:

> *Before reading:* where students are encouraged to reflect on the theme of the story prior to reading and perhaps predict what might happen.

> *During reading:* where students are encouraged to reflect on how the story is developing and perhaps consider what might happen next.

> *After reading:* where students are given the opportunity of responding to the story through a variety of talking and writing assignments.

Teachers using the collection are therefore recommended to preview the 'Follow On' section before reading the stories with students.

Gervase Phinn

DORIS LESSING

No Witchcraft for Sale

The Farquars had been childless for years when little Teddy was born; and they were touched by the pleasure of their servants, who brought presents of fowls and eggs and flowers to the homestead when they came to rejoice over the baby, exclaiming with delight over his downy golden head and his blue eyes. They congratulated Mrs Farquar as if she had achieved a very great thing, and she felt that she had — her smile for the lingering, admiring natives was warm and grateful.

Later, when Teddy had his first haircut, Gideon the cook picked up the soft gold tufts from the ground, and held them reverently in his hand. Then he smiled at the little boy and said: 'Little Yellow Head'. That became the native name for the child. Gideon and Teddy were great friends from the first. When Gideon had finished his work, he would lift Teddy on his shoulders to the shade of a big tree, and play with him there, forming curious little toys from twigs and leaves and grass, or shaping animals from wetted soil. When Teddy learned to walk it was often Gideon who crouched before him, clucking encouragement, finally catching him when he fell, tossing him up in the air till they both became breathless with laughter. Mrs Farquar was fond of the old cook because of his love for her child.

There was no second baby; and one day Gideon said: 'Ah,

missus, missus, the Lord above sent this one; Little Yellow
Head is the most good thing we have in our house.' Because of
that 'we' Mrs Farquar felt a warm impulse towards her cook;
and at the end of the month she raised his wages. He had been
with her now for several years; he was one of the few natives
who had his wife and children in the compound and never
wanted to go home to his kraal, which was some hundreds of
miles away. Sometimes a small piccanin, who had been born the
same time as Teddy, could be seen peering from the edge of the
bush, staring in awe at the little white boy with his miraculous
fair hair and northern blue eyes. The two little children would
gaze at each other with a wide interested gaze, and once Teddy
put out his hand curiously to touch the black child's cheeks and
hair.

Gideon, who was watching, shook his head wonderingly, and
said: 'Ah, missus, these are both children, and one will grow up
to be a Baas, and one will be a servant'; and Mrs Farquar smiled
and said sadly, 'Yes, Gideon, I was thinking the same.' She
sighed. 'It is God's will,' said Gideon, who was a mission boy.
The Farquars were very religious people; and this shared feeling
about God bound servant and masters even closer together.

Teddy was about six years old when he was given a scooter,
and discovered the intoxications of speed. All day he would fly
around the homestead, in and out of flowerbeds, scattering
squawking chickens and irritated dogs, finishing with a wide
dizzying arc into the kitchen door. There he would cry: 'Gideon,
look at me!' And Gideon would laugh and say: 'Very clever,
Little Yellow Head.' Gideon's youngest son, who was now a
herdsboy, came especially up from the compound to see the
scooter. He was afraid to come near it, but Teddy showed off in
front of him. 'Piccanin,' shouted Teddy, 'get out of my way!'
And he raced in circles around the black child until he was
frightened, and fled back to the bush.

'Why did you frighten him?' asked Gideon, gravely reproachful.

Teddy said defiantly: 'He's only a black boy,' and laughed.
Then, when Gideon turned away from him without speaking,
his face fell. Very soon he slipped into the house and found an
orange and brought it to Gideon, saying: 'This is for you.' He
could not bring himself to say he was sorry; but he could not

bear to lose Gideon's affection either. Gideon took the orange unwillingly and sighed. 'Soon you will be going away to school, Little Yellow Head,' he said wonderingly, 'and then you will be grown up.' He shook his head gently and said, 'And that is how our lives go.' He seemed to be putting a distance between himself and Teddy, not because of resentment, but in the way a person accepts something inevitable. The baby had lain in his arms and smiled up into his face: the tiny boy had swung from his shoulders, had played with him by the hour. Now Gideon would not let his flesh touch the flesh of the white child. He was kind, but there was a grave formality in his voice that made Teddy pout and sulk away. Also, it made him into a man: with Gideon he was polite, and carried himself formally, and if he came into the kitchen to ask for something, it was in the way a white man uses towards a servant, expecting to be obeyed.

But on the day that Teddy came staggering into the kitchen with his fists to his eyes, shrieking with pain, Gideon dropped the pot full of hot soup that he was holding, rushed to the child, and forced aside his fingers. 'A snake!' he exclaimed. Teddy had been on his scooter, and had come to a rest with his foot on the side of a big tub full of plants. A tree-snake, hanging by its tail from the roof, had spat full into his eyes. Mrs Farquar came running when she heard the commotion. 'He'll go blind,' she sobbed, holding Teddy close against her. 'Gideon, he'll go blind!' Already the eyes, with perhaps half an hour's sight left in them, were swollen up to the size of fists: Teddy's small white face was distorted by great purple oozing protuberances. Gideon said: 'Wait a minute, missus, I'll get some medicine.' He ran off into the bush. Mrs Farquar lifted the child into the house and bathed his eyes with permanganate. She had scarcely heard Gideon's words; but when she saw that her remedies had no effect at all, and remembered how she had seen natives with no sight in their eyes, because of the spitting of a snake, she began to look for the return of her cook, remembering what she had heard of the efficacy of native herbs. She stood by the window, holding the terrified, sobbing little boy in her arms, and peered helplessly into the bush. It was not more than a few minutes before she saw Gideon come bounding back, and in his hand he held a plant.

'Do not be afraid, missus,' said Gideon, 'this will cure Little Yellow Head's eyes.' He stripped the leaves from the plant, leaving a small white fleshy root. Without even washing it, he put the root in his mouth, chewed it vigorously, and then held the spittle there while he took the child forcibly from Mrs Farquar. He gripped Teddy down between his knees, and pressed the balls of his thumbs into the swollen eyes, so that the child screamed and Mrs Farquar cried out in protest: 'Gideon, Gideon!' But Gideon took no notice. He knelt over the writhing child, pushing back the puffy lids till chinks of eyeball showed, and then he spat hard, again and again, into first one eye, and then the other. He finally lifted Teddy gently into his mother's arms, and said: 'His eyes will get better.' But Mrs Farquar was weeping with terror, and she could hardly thank him: it was impossible to believe that Teddy could keep his sight. In a couple of hours the swellings were gone; the eyes were inflamed and tender but Teddy could see. Mr and Mrs Farquar went to Gideon in the kitchen and thanked him over and over again. They felt helpless because of their gratitude: it seemed they could do nothing to express it. They gave Gideon presents for his wife and children, and a big increase in wages, but these things could not pay for Teddy's now completely cured eyes. Mrs Farquar said: 'Gideon, God chose you as an instrument for His goodness,' and Gideon said: 'Yes, missus, God is very good.'

Now, when such a thing happens on a farm, it cannot be long before everyone hears of it. Mr and Mrs Farquar told their neighbours and the story was discussed from one end of the district to the other. The bush is full of secrets. No one can live in Africa, or at least on the veld, without learning very soon that there is an ancient wisdom of leaf and soil and season — and, too, perhaps most important of all, of the darker tracts of the human mind — which is the black man's heritage. Up and down the district people were telling anecdotes, reminding each other of things that had happened to them.

'But I saw it myself, I tell you. It was a puff-adder bite. The kaffir's arm was swollen to the elbow, like a great shiny black bladder. He was groggy after half a minute. He was dying. Then suddenly a kaffir walked out of the bush with his hands full of green stuff. He smeared something on the place, and next day my boy was back at work, and all you could see was two small punctures in the skin.'

This was the kind of tale they told. And, as always, with a certain amount of exasperation, because while all of them knew that in the bush of Africa are waiting valuable drugs locked in bark, in simple-looking leaves, in roots, it was impossible to ever get the truth about them from the natives themselves.

The story eventually reached town; and perhaps it was at a sundowner party, or some such function, that a doctor, who happened to be there, challenged it. 'Nonsense,' he said. 'These things get exaggerated in the telling. We are always checking up on this kind of story, and we draw a blank every time.'

Anyway, one morning there arrived a strange car at the homestead, and out stepped one of the workers from the laboratory in town, with cases full of test-tubes and chemicals.

Mr and Mrs Farquar were flustered and pleased and flattered. They asked the scientist to lunch, and they told the story all over again, for the hundredth time. Little Teddy was there too, his blue eyes sparkling with health, to prove the truth of it. The scientist explained how humanity might benefit if this new drug could be offered for sale; and the Farquars were even more pleased: they were kind, simple people, who liked to think of something good coming about because of them. But when the scientist began talking of the money that might result, their manner showed discomfort. Their feelings over the miracle (that was how they thought of it) were so strong and deep and religious, that it was distasteful to them to think of money. The scientist, seeing their faces, went back to his first point, which was the advancement of humanity. He was perhaps a trifle perfunctory: it was not the first time he had come salting the tail of a fabulous bush-secret.

Eventually, when the meal was over, the Farquars called Gideon into their living-room and explained to him that this baas, here, was a Big Doctor from the Big City, and he had come all that way to see Gideon. At this Gideon seemed afraid; he did not understand; and Mrs Farquar explained quickly that it was because of the wonderful thing he had done with Teddy's eyes that the Big Baas had come.

Gideon looked from Mrs Farquar to Mr Farquar, and then at
the little boy, who was showing great importance because of the
occasion. At last he said grudgingly: 'The Big Baas wants to
know what medicine I used?' He spoke incredulously, as if he
could not believe his old friends could so betray him. Mr
Farquar began explaining how a useful medicine could be made
out of the root, and how it could be put on sale, and how
thousands of people, black and white, up and down the continent
of Africa, could be saved by the medicine when that spitting
snake filled their eyes with poison. Gideon listened, his eyes
bent on the ground, the skin of his forehead puckering in
discomfort. When Mr Farquar had finished he did not reply.
The scientist, who all this time had been leaning back in a big
chair, sipping his coffee and smiling with sceptical good-humour,
chipped in and explained all over again, in different words,
about the making of drugs and the progress of science. Also, he
offered Gideon a present.

There was a silence after this further explanation, and then
Gideon remarked indifferently that he could not remember the
root. His face was sullen and hostile, even when he looked at
the Farquars, whom he usually treated like old friends. They
were beginning to feel annoyed; and this feeling annulled the
guilt that had been sprung into life by Gideon's accusing manner.
They were beginning to feel that he was unreasonable. But it
was at that moment that they all realised he would never give in.
The magical drug would remain where it was, unknown and
useless except for the tiny scattering of Africans who had the
knowledge, natives who might be digging a ditch for the munici-
pality in a ragged shirt and a pair of patched shorts, but who
were still born to healing, hereditary healers, being the nephews
or sons of the old witch doctors whose ugly masks and bits of
bone and all the uncouth properties of magic were the outward
signs of real power and wisdom.

The Farquars might tread on that plant fifty times a day as
they passed from house to garden, from cow kraal to mealie
field, but they would never know it.

But they went on persuading and arguing, with all the force
of their exasperation; and Gideon continued to say that he
could not remember, or that there was no such root, or that it

was the wrong season of the year, or that it wasn't the root itself but the spittle from his mouth that had cured Teddy's eyes. He said all these things one after another, and seemed not to care they were contradictory. He was rude and stubborn. The Farquars could hardly recognise their gentle, lovable old servant in this ignorant, perversely obstinate native, standing there in front of them with lowered eyes, his hands twitching his cook's apron, repeating over and over whichever one of the stupid refusals that first entered his head.

And suddenly he appeared to give in. He lifted his head, gave a long, blank angry look at the circle of whites, who seemed to him like a circle of yelping dogs pressing around him, and said: 'I will show you the root.'

They walked single file away from the homestead down a kaffir path. It was a blazing December afternoon, with the sky full of hot rain-clouds. Everything was hot: the sun was like a bronze tray whirling overhead, there was a heat shimmer over the fields, the soil was scorching underfoot, the dusty wind blew gritty and thick and warm in their faces. It was a terrible day, fit only for reclining on a verandah with iced drinks, which is where they would normally have been at that hour.

From time to time, remembering that on the day of the snake it had taken ten minutes to find the root, someone asked: 'Is it much further, Gideon?' And Gideon would answer over his shoulder, with angry politeness: 'I'm looking for the root, baas.' And indeed, he would frequently bend sideways and trail his hand among the grasses with a gesture that was insulting in its perfunctoriness. He walked them through the bush along unknown paths for two hours, in that melting destroying heat, so that the sweat trickled coldly down them and their heads ached. They were all quite silent: the Farquars because they were angry, the scientist because he was being proved right again; there was no such plant. His was a tactful silence.

At last, six miles from the house, Gideon suddenly decided they had had enough; or perhaps his anger evaporated at that moment. He picked up, without an attempt at looking anything but casual, a handful of blue flowers from the grass, flowers that had been growing plentifully all down the paths they had come.

He handed them to the scientist without looking at him, and

marched off by himself on the way home, leaving them to follow him if they chose.

When they got back to the house, the scientist went to the kitchen to thank Gideon: he was being very polite, even though there was an amused look in his eyes. Gideon was not there. Throwing the flowers causually into the back of his car, the eminent visitor departed on his way back to his laboratory.

Gideon was back in his kitchen in time to prepare dinner, but he was sulking. He spoke to Mrs Farquar like an unwilling servant. It was days before they liked each other again.

The Farquars made enquiries about the root from their labourers. Sometimes they were answered with distrustful stares. Sometimes the natives said: 'We do not know. We have never heard of the root.' One, the cattle boy, who had been with them a long time, and had grown to trust them a little, said: 'Ask your boy in the kitchen. Now, there's a doctor for you. He's the son of a famous medicine man who used to be in these parts, and there's nothing he cannot cure.' Then he added politely: 'Of course, he's not as good as the white man's doctor, we know that, but he's good for us.'

After some time, when the soreness had gone from between the Farquars and Gideon, they began to joke: 'When are you going to show us the snake-root, Gideon?' And he would laugh and shake his head, saying, a little uncomfortably: 'But I did show you, missus, have you forgotten?'

Much later, Teddy, as a schoolboy, would come into the kitchen and say: 'You old rascal, Gideon! Do you remember that time you tricked us all by making us walk miles all over the veld for nothing? It was so far my father had to carry me!'

And Gideon would double up with polite laughter. After much laughing, he would suddenly straighten himself up, wipe his old eyes, and look sadly at Teddy, who was grinning mischievously at him across the kitchen: 'Ah, Little Yellow Head, how you have grown! Soon you will be grown up with a farm of your own . . .'

MIKE HAYWOOD

The Rose Garden

Charlie Brown. It's not a complicated name but it's unique like all names. Charlie Brown, tall with a slight stoop, about six feet, three inches. Green eyes and a tanned face that turns pale in the evening from too much smoking or not enough sleep.

Charlie is a moving man. He doesn't stay too long in any one place. Few real painters do. They follow their nose to a site, have a look round, find out if the money is above the union rate and if it is, that's good enough.

He's a union man all the same. Charlie moves, but the union card stays in a zip pocket of the tool bag. By the end of the year it gets a bit grubby but it's always renewed. You can't stand alone all the time. Sometimes you have to turn to authority even if it's your own authority for your own ends. And not for any social ideas.

When challenged he admits he's 'a socialist of sorts', but more often than that he leaves it at that.

It's after five. It's winter and it's raining. You don't work the site when it's this bad. The paint won't hold. Sometimes it's workable when it's wet. A lot depends on the boss man. Some have principles, some don't. The ones that don't let you dry things with a blow lamp and bash on a few coats. Next summer it peels like mad. But you've gone with the money by then. A lot depends on principles. Some bosses don't need principles. Others do.

After five. And it's raining. Buses go by full of people. Steamed up windows. Women with shopping and wet boots. Wet handbags and wet macs. Clutching the *Evening Star* — the thing that tells you what the government is going to cut down on next — which member of the Royalty is in the family way — and what Alderman Strickland said about comprehensive schools abolishing the eleven plus and why he's putting up the rates — because we're all so prosperous now.

That's all in the steamed up buses with wage packets being opened to pay the fare with pounds. Damp pounds. It's money anyway. Maybe you stood in a queue and waited for it. Maybe somebody brought it to your desk. But it's money. Charlie didn't get a big drag this week. Bugger the rain. That's a price he pays for being a painter. For being a moving man.

Up through the fog came the 96. Charlie walked slowly along with the others. Clutching his tool bag. It's a good tool bag. The tools always clean. Scrapers, sign writing brushes in a neat polished tin box. Perfect brushes made of the best bristle. On the lid is an inscription 'To Charlie Brown from the School of Art and Craft, 1949'. He took all the prizes that year. He's a craftsman to the last bristle. He walks slowly along seeing nobody.

The bus stopped. And these new automatic doors let him into the steamy warmth. He went upstairs. He always goes upstairs. Then when the bus gets full you don't have to give your seat to some old woman, who you ought to feel sorry for, or who you have to pretend to feel sorry for. Because somebody or everybody is looking at you that way.

Or if you stand up for a young bit she might think you're trying it on, and maybe you are. So it's best to go upstairs even if it does smell a bit.

Well it can't be otherwise when you think there's maybe twenty or thirty steel-workers up there who clocked out without getting washed all over. After eight or twelve hours in a mill. When maybe they've been gobbling fumes and such all day. They get on the bus and light fags like looneys. It doesn't smell exactly like a rose garden or a tart's bedroom.

Maybe it's their first decent smoke all day. In a mill fags taste like old rag. They get black with your fingers. Taste horrible.

On the bus your hands could still be black but they taste better. Maybe it's just the freedom that makes them better. You can't enjoy a fag when there's a foreman and managers and lackeys creeping around all over the place. Sometimes you have to leave your fag on the edge of a machine, or on a bench and it gets oily that way. Gives you cancer quicker. Nearly as quick as the fumes you've been gobbling all day.

No. It's no Rose Garden up here on top of this bus. What do you expect? The roses have been cut back too early. They've got chopped by the frost. Gone all snarled up. Grown old too early. Or gone wild again. The lucky ones go wild again. Ramble away all over. Get out of control. Like a moving man.

Charlie remembered his old man.

'When tha leaves school tha mon come wi' me to mill.'

Charlie had said nothing. He'd reached across the table for another tomato.

'Can you hear your Dad or not?' his mother had said.

He'd stayed silent a bit. Cutting the tomato and reaching out for some bread.

She was a tall woman, with a long nose and a pale intelligent face. Thin and flat-chested.

Charlie had carved the tomato and laid the slices across the bread. He hadn't replied.

'Well swallowed your bloody tongue, or summat?' the old man questioned.

Another silence.

'I'm going painting,' Charlie announced at last. 'It looks a nice job, does painting.'

They didn't argue. No good with Charlie. But they didn't like it.

The other brothers went to the mill to do what they wanted. And Charlie went his way to do what he wanted.

The old lady didn't like having not much money from him, she told him so. But it was said she bragged a bit in the butcher's about him being a tradesman who could start up on his own one day.

'If you've got to work, you might as well work for yourself.'

Charlie never did that either. Just changed bosses when he felt like it.

'Hey up, young fella, does tha want all this seat?'

The voice shook Charlie out of his thought. He looked sideways to see a little chap with a dusty face and no teeth.

The bus was standing. It seemed it would never move. Standing trapped in the traffic. Same every night. Solve the traffic problem when everybody wants a flipping car.

That's what the little chap was saying anyway. Sitting and stamping his feet and rubbing hard on the steamy window with his sleeve.

'Where are we?' said Charlie. 'Not out of the city yet, mate.'

'Progress, progress, that's progress closing the railways, filling up the canals.' The little chap kept going on and nudging Charlie with his elbow inviting argument.

'Tavitt Lane, Bloody Hell, never get home,' he continued.

'I'm in no hurry,' said Charlie. 'You going somewhere?'

'Home, home,' said the little chap. 'I want my tea.'

'Mine can wait,' Charlie grinned. 'I'm in no hurry, it's my landlady's night out. She always plays Bingo on Fridays. So I get some chips or a few pickled onions.'

'That wouldn't do for me. I like something waiting good and hot, something decent. I'm not one for catch penny suppers — not me,' were the little chap's last words as he made for the top of the stairs.

With relief Charlie spread himself once more on the full width of the seat.

'Terminus.'

He gathered the tool bag and stepped onto the wet pavement. And walked quickly to the swing doors beckoning from across the street.

The beer was good tonight. That makes a change. At 9.30 he decided it was time for his chips.

In the chip-shop Charlie saw the little chap. He looked tired and hungry. His eyes were wet, not with the rain, but with weeping.

Charlie leaned on the park railings. Looked a long time at the roses and at last moved on.

NIGEL KNEALE

The Pond

It was deeply scooped from a corner of the field, a green stagnant hollow with thorn bushes on its banks.

From time to time something moved cautiously beneath the prickly branches that were laden with red autumn berries. It whistled and murmured coaxingly.

'Come, come, come, come,' it whispered. An old man, squatting frog-like on the bank. His words were no louder than the rustling of the dry leaves above his head. 'Come now. Sssst — ssst! Little dear — here's a bit of meat for thee.' He tossed a tiny scrap of something into the pool. The weed rippled sluggishly.

The old man sighed and shifted his position. He was crouching on his haunches because the bank was damp.

He froze.

The green slime had parted on the far side of the pool. The disturbance travelled to the bank opposite, and a large frog drew itself half out of the water. It stayed quite still, watching; then with a swift crawl it was clear of the water. Its yellow throat throbbed.

'Oh! — little dear,' breathed the old man. He did not move.

He waited, letting the frog grow accustomed to the air and slippery earth. When he judged the moment to be right, he made a low grating noise in his throat.

He saw the frog listen.

The sound was subtly like the call of its own kind. The old man paused, then made it again.

This time the frog answered. It sprang into the pool, sending the green weed slopping, and swam strongly. Only its eyes showed above the water. It crawled out a few feet distant from the old man and looked up the bank, as if eager to find the frog it had heard.

The old man waited patiently. The frog hopped twice, up the bank.

His hand was moving, so slowly that it did not seem to move, towards the handle of the light net at his side. He gripped it, watching the still frog.

Suddenly he struck.

A sweep of the net, and its wire frame whacked the ground about the frog. It leaped frantically, but was helpless in the green mesh.

'Dear! Oh, my dear!' said the old man delightedly.

He stood with much difficulty and pain, his foot on the thin rod. His joints had stiffened and it was some minutes before he could go to the net. The frog was still struggling desperately. He closed the net round its body and picked both up together.

'Ah, big beauty!' he said. 'Pretty. Handsome fellow, you!'

He took a darning needle from his coat lapel and carefully killed the creature through the mouth, so that its skin would not be damaged; then put it in his pocket.

It was the last frog in the pond.

He lashed the water with the handle, and the weed swirled and bobbed: there was no sign of life now but the little flies that flitted on the surface.

He went across the empty field with the net across his shoulder, shivering a little, feeling that the warmth had gone out of his body during the long wait. He climbed a stile, throwing the net over in front of him, to leave his hands free. In the next field, by the road, was his cottage.

Hobbling through the grass with the sun striking a long shadow from him, he felt the weight of the dead frog in his pocket, and was glad.

'Big beauty!' he murmured again.

The cottage was small and dry, and ugly and very old. Its

windows gave little light, and they had coloured panels, dark-blue and green, that gave the rooms the appearance of being under the sea.

The old man lit a lamp, for the sun had set; and the light became more cheerful. He put the frog on a plate, and poked the fire, and when he was warm again, took off his coat.

He settled down close beside the lamp and took a sharp knife from the drawer of the table. With great care and patience, he began to skin the frog.

From time to time he took off his spectacles and rubbed his eyes. The work was tiring; also the heat from the lamp made them sore. He would speak aloud to the dead creature, coaxing and cajoling it when he found his task difficult. But in time he had the skin neatly removed, a little heap of tumbled, slippery film. He dropped the stiff, stripped body into a pan of boiling water on the fire, and sat again, humming and fingering the limp skin.

'Pretty,' he said. 'You'll be so handsome.'

There was a stump of black soap in the drawer and he took it out to rub the skin, with the slow, over-careful motion that showed the age in his hand. The little mottled thing began to stiffen under the curing action. He left it at last, and brewed himself a pot of tea, lifting the lid of the simmering pan occasionally to make sure that the tiny skull and bones were being boiled clean without damage.

Sipping his tea, he crossed the narrow living-room. Well away from the fire stood a high table, its top covered by a square of dark cloth supported on a frame. There was a faint smell of decay.

'How are you, little dears?' said the old man.

He lifted the covering with shaky scrupulousness. Beneath the wire support were dozens of stuffed frogs.

All had been posed in human attitudes; dressed in tiny coats and breeches to the fashion of an earlier time. There were ladies and gentlemen and bowing flunkeys. One, with lace at his yellow, waxen throat, held a wooden wine-cup. To the dried forepaw of its neighbour was stitched a tiny glassless monocle, raised to a black button eye. A third had a midget pipe pressed into its jaws, with a wisp of wool for smoke. The same coarse wool, cleaned and shaped, served the ladies for their miniature wigs; they wore long skirts and carried fans.

The old man looked proudly over the stiff little figures.

'You, my lord — what are you doing, with your mouth so glum?' His fingers prised open the jaws of a round-bellied frog dressed in satins; shrinkage must have closed them. 'Now you can sing again, and drink up!'

His eyes searched the banqueting, motionless party.

'Where now—? Ah!'

In the middle of the table three of the creatures were fixed in the attitudes of a dance.

The old man spoke to them. 'Soon we'll have a partner for the lady there. He'll be the handsomest of the whole company, my dear, so don't forget to smile at him and look your prettiest!'

He hurried back to the fireplace and lifted the pan; poured off the steaming water into a bucket.

'Fine, shapely brain-box you have.' He picked with his knife, cleaning the tiny skull. 'Easy does it.' He put it down on the table, admiringly; it was like a transparent flake of ivory. One by one he found the delicate bones in the pan, knowing each for what it was.

'Now, little duke, we have all of them that we need,' he said at last. 'We can make you into a picture indeed. The beau of the ball. And such an object of jealousy for the lovely ladies!'

With wire and thread he fashioned a stiff little skeleton, binding in the bones to preserve the proportions. At the top went the skull.

The frog's skin had lost its earlier flaccidness. He threaded a needle, eyeing it close to the lamp. From the table drawer he now brought a loose wad of wool. Like a doctor reassuring his patient by describing his methods, he began to talk.

'This wool is coarse, I know, little friend. A poor substitute to fill that skin of yours, you may say: wool from the hedges, snatched by the thorns from a sheep's back.' He was pulling the wad into tufts of the size he required. 'But you'll find it gives you such a springiness that you'll thank me for it. Now, carefully does it—'

With perfect concentration he worked his needle through the skin, drawing it together round the wool with almost untraceable stitches.

'A piece of lace in your left hand, or shall it be a quizzing-glass?' With tiny scissors he trimmed away a fragment of skin. 'But wait — it's a dance and it is your right hand that we must see, guiding the lady.'

He worked the skin precisely into place round the skull. He would attend to the empty eye-holes later.

Suddenly he lowered his needle.

He listened.

Puzzled, he put down the half-stuffed skin and went to the door and opened it.

The sky was dark now. He heard the sound more clearly. He knew it was coming from the pond. A far-off, harsh croaking, as of a great many frogs.

He frowned.

In the wall cupboard he found a lantern ready trimmed, and lit it with a flickering splinter. He put on an overcoat and hat, remembering his earlier chill. Lastly he took his net.

He went very cautiously. His eyes saw nothing at first, after working so close to the lamp. Then, as the croaking came to him more clearly and he grew accustomed to the darkness, he hurried.

He climbed the stile as before, throwing the net ahead. This time, however, he had to search for it in the darkness, tantalised by the sounds from the pond. When it was in his hand again, he began to move stealthily.

About twenty yards from the pool he stopped and listened.

There was no wind and the noise astonished him. Hundreds of frogs must have travelled through the fields to this spot; from other water where danger had arisen, perhaps, or drought. He had heard of such instances.

Almost on tiptoe he crept towards the pond. He could see nothing yet. There was no moon, and the thorn bushes hid the surface of the water.

He was a few paces from the pond when, without warning, every sound ceased.

He froze again. There was absolute silence. Not even a watery plop or splashing told that one frog out of all those hundreds had dived for shelter into the weed. It was strange.

He stepped forward, and heard his boots brushing the grass.

He brought the net up across his chest, ready to strike if he saw anything move. He came to the thorn bushes, and still heard no sound. Yet, to judge by the noise they had made, they should be hopping in dozens from beneath his feet.

Peering, he made the throaty noise which had called the frog that afternoon. The hush continued.

He looked down at where the water must be. The surface of the pond, shadowed by the bushes, was too dark to be seen. He shivered, and waited.

Gradually, as he stood, he became aware of a smell.

It was wholly unpleasant. Seemingly it came from the weed, yet mixed with the vegetable odour was one of another kind of decay. A soft, oozy bubbling accompanied it. Gases must be rising from the mud at the bottom. It would not do to stay in this place and risk his health.

He stooped, still puzzled by the disappearance of the frogs, and stared once more at the dark surface. Pulling his net to a ready position, he tried the throaty call for the last time.

Instantly he threw himself backwards with a cry.

A vast, belching bubble of foul air shot from the pool. Another gushed up past his head; then another. Great patches of slimy weed were flung high among the thorn branches.

The whole pond seemed to boil.

He turned blindly to escape, and stepped into the thorns. He was in agony. A dreadful slobbering deafened his ears: the stench overcame his senses. He felt the net whipped from his hand. The icy weeds were wet on his face. Reeds lashed him.

Then he was in the midst of an immense, pulsating softness that yielded and received and held him. He knew he was shrieking. He knew there was no one to hear him.

An hour after the sun had risen, the rain slackened to a light drizzle.

A policeman cycled slowly on the road that ran by the cottage, shaking out his cape with one hand, and half-expecting the old man to appear and call out a comment on the weather. Then he caught sight of the lamp, still burning feebly in the kitchen, and dismounted. He found the door ajar, and wondered if something was wrong.

He called to the old man. He saw the uncommon handiwork lying on the table as if it had been suddenly dropped; and the unused bed.

For half an hour the policeman searched in the neighbourhood of the cottage, calling out the old man's name at intervals, before remembering the pond. He turned towards the stile.

Climbing over it, he frowned and began to hurry. He was disturbed by what he saw.

On the bank of the pond crouched a naked figure.

The policeman went closer. He saw it was the old man, on his haunches; his arms were straight; the hands resting between his feet. He did not move as the policeman approached.

'Hallo, there!' said the policeman. He ducked to avoid the thorn bushes catching his helmet. 'This won't do, you know. You can get into trouble—'

He saw green slime in the old man's beard, and the staring eyes. His spine chilled. With an unprofessional distaste, he quickly put out a hand and took the old man by the upper arm. It was cold. He shivered, and moved the arm gently.

Then he groaned and ran from the pond.

For the arm had come away at the shoulder: reeds and green water-plants and slime tumbled from the broken joint.

As the old man fell backwards, tiny green stitches glistened across his belly.

H. E. BATES

The Goat and the Stars

Every morning, when he came into the town, going to school, he would see this large and to him discomforting notice in blue and scarlet letters on a board outside the church. It had been there since a month before Christmas. 'Annual Collection of Christmas Gifts in this Church on Christmas Eve. Help Us to Help Others. No Gift too Large. None too Small. Give generously.' And then, in very much larger, startling and to him almost angry letters: 'THIS MEANS YOU!'

He was a small, extremely puzzled-looking boy with a look of searching determination on his rather thin lips. Large brown trousers, which looked as if they had been cut down from his father's, gave him a curious look of being out of place in the world. His hair looked as if it had been shorn off with sheep shears; his forehead had in it small, constant knots of perplexity. There was always mud on his boots and, though he did not know it, there were times when he did not smell very sweet.

There was a reason for this smell. His father and mother had a small farm-holding of about ten acres two miles out in the country. On a little pasture they grazed a mare and two or three cows, with a score of foraging hens. Outside the house ran a wide strip of roadside verge, and here they grazed a dozen goats. It was because of the goats that the boy sometimes created a very pungent and startling impression. He was very

26

fond of the goats and it was his job to tether them on the roadside grass every morning and again, if he were home before darkness fell, to house them up in the disused pigsty for the night. He treated the goats like friends. He knew that they were his friends. At frequent intervals the number of goats was increased, but his father could never sell the kids or even give them away. The boy was always glad about this and now they had thirteen goats: the odd one a kid of six weeks, all white, as pure as snow.

Every morning when he went by the church the notice had some power of making him uneasy. It was the challenge in larger letters, THIS MEANS YOU! that troubled him. More and more, as Christmas came near, he got into the habit of worrying about it. The notice seemed to spring out and hit him in the face; it seemed to make a hole in his conscience. It singled him out from the rest of the world: THIS MEANS YOU!

Soon, as he walked down from the country in the mornings and then back again in the evenings, he began to think if there was anything he could do about it. It seemed to him that he had to do something. The notice, as time went on, made him feel as if it were watching him. Once he had heard a story in which there had been a repetitive phrase which had also troubled him: God Sees All. Gradually he got into his head the idea that in addition to the notice God, too, was watching him. In a way God and the notice were one.

It was not until the day before Christmas Eve that he decided to give the goat-kid to the church. He woke up with the decision lying, as it were, in his hands. It was as if it had been made for him and he knew that there was no escaping it.

He had already grown deeply fond of the little goat and it seemed to him a very great thing to sacrifice. That day there was no school and he spent most of the afternoon in the pigsty, kneeling on the strawed floor, combing the delicate milky hair of the little goat with a horse comb. In the sty the powerful congested smell of goats was solid, but he did not notice it. It had long since penetrated his body and whatever clothes he wore.

By the time he had finished brushing and combing the goat he had begun to feel extremely proud and glad of it; he had begun to get the idea that no other gift would be quite so beautiful. He did not know what other people would give. No gift was too great, none too small, and perhaps people would give things like oranges and nuts, perhaps things like toys and Christmas trees. There was no telling what would be given. He only knew that no one else would give quite what he was giving: something small and beautiful and living, that was his friend.

When the goat-kid was ready he tied a piece of clean string round its neck and tethered it to a ring in the pigsty. His plan for taking it down into the town was simple. Every Christmas Eve he had to go and visit an aunt who kept a small corner grocery store in the town, and this aunt would give him a box of dates for his father, a box of chocolates for his mother and some sort of present for himself. All he had to do was to take the kid with him under cover of darkness. It was so light that he could carry it in his hands.

He got down into the town just before 7 o'clock. Round the goat he had tied a clean meal-sack, in case of rain. When the goat grew tired of walking he would carry it in his arms; then when he got tired of carrying it the goat would walk again. Only one thing troubled him. He did not know what the procedure at the church would be. There might, he imagined, be a long sort of desk, with men in charge. He would go to this desk and say, very simply, 'I have brought this,' and come away.

He was rather disconcerted to find the windows of the church full of light. He saw people, carrying parcels, going through the door. He saw the notice, a little torn by weather now, but still flaring at him: THIS MEANS YOU! and he felt slightly nervous as he stood on the other side of the street, with the kid at his side, on the string, like a little dog.

Finally when there were no more people going into the church and it was very quiet he decided to go in. After taking the sacking off the kid he took it into his arms, smoothing its hair into place with the nervous tips of his fingers.

When he went into the church he was surprised to find it almost full of people. There was already a sort of service in progress and he sat hastily down at the end of a pew, seeing at the other end of the church, in the soft light of candles, a reconstruction of the manger and Child and the Wise Men who had followed the moving star. The stable and its manger reminded him of the pigsty where the goats were kept, and his first impression was that it would be a good sleeping-place for the kid.

He sat for some minutes before anything happened. A clergyman, speaking from the pulpit, was talking of the grace of giving. 'They,' he said, 'brought frankincense and myrrh! You cannot bring frankincense, but what you have brought has a sweeter smell: the smell of sacrifice for others.'

As he spoke a man immediately in front of the boy turned to his wife, sniffing, and then whispering:

'Funny smell of frankincense.'

'Yes,' she whispered. She too was sniffing now. 'I noticed it but didn't like to say.'

They began to sniff together, like dogs. After some moments the woman turned and saw the boy, sitting tense and nervous, the knots of perplexity tight on his forehead and the goat in his arms.

'Look round!' she said.

The man turned and now he too saw the goat.

'Well!' he said. 'Well, no wonder!'

'I hate them,' the woman whispered. 'I hate that smell.'

They began sniffing now with deliberation, attracting the attention of other people, who too turned and saw the goat. In the pews about the boy there was a flutter of suppressed consternation. Finally, at the instigation of his wife, the man in front of the boy got up and went out.

He returned a minute later with an usher. Before going back to his pew he whispered:

'There. My wife can't stand the smell.'

A moment later the usher was whispering into the boy's ear, 'I'm afraid it's hardly the right place for this. I'm afraid you'll have to go out.' At the approach of a strange person the little goat began to struggle, and suddenly let out a thin bleat of alarm. As the boy got up it seemed to him that the whole church turned and looked at him partly in amusement, partly alarm, as though the presence of the kid were on the fringe of sacrilege.

Outside, the usher pointed down the steps. 'All right, son, you run along.'

'I wanted to give the goat,' the boy said.

'Yes, I know,' the man said, 'but you got the wrong idea. A goat's no use to anybody.'

The boy walked down the steps of the church into the street, the goat quiet now in his arms. He did not look at the notice which had said for so long THIS MEANS YOU! because it was clear to him now that he had made a sort of mistake. It was clear that the notice did not mean him at all.

Outside the town he walked slowly in the darkness. The night air was silent and the kid seemed almost asleep in his arms. He was not now troubled that they did not want the goat, but was already glad that it would be his again.

It was only by some other things that he was troubled. He had for a long time believed that at Christmas there must be snow on the ground, and bells ringing, and a moving star.

But now there was no snow on the ground. There were no bells ringing, and far above himself and the little goat the stars were still.

KATE CHOPIN

Désirée's Baby

As the day was pleasant, Madame Valmondé drove over to L'Abri to see Désirée and the baby.

It made her laugh to think of Désirée with a baby. Why, it seemed but yesterday that Désirée was little more than a baby herself; when Monsieur in riding through the gateway of Valmondé had found her lying asleep in the shadow of the big stone pillar.

The little one awoke in his arms and began to cry for 'Dada'. That was as much as she could do or say. Some people thought she might have strayed there of her own accord, for she was of the toddling age. The prevailing belief was that she had been purposely left by a party of Texans, whose canvas-covered wagon, late in the day, had crossed the ferry that Coton Mais kept, just below the plantation. In time Madame Valmondé abandoned every speculation but the one that Désirée had been sent to her by a beneficent Providence to be the child of her affection, seeing that she was without child of the flesh. For the girl grew to be beautiful and gentle, affectionate and sincere, — the idol of Valmondé.

It was no wonder, when she stood one day against the stone pillar in whose shadow she had lain asleep, eighteen years before, that Armand Aubigny riding by and seeing her there, had fallen in love with her. That was the way all the Aubignys fell in love, as if struck by a pistol shot. The wonder was that he had not loved her before; for he had known her since his father brought him home from Paris, a boy of eight, after his mother died there. The passion that awoke in him that day, when he saw her at the gate, swept along like an avalanche, or like a prairie fire, or like anything that drives headlong over all obstacles.

Monsieur Valmondé grew practical and wanted things well considered: that is, the girl's obscure origin. Armand looked into her eyes and did not care. He was reminded that she was nameless. What did it matter about a name when he could give her one of the oldest and proudest in Louisiana? He ordered the *corbeille* from Paris, and contained himself with what patience he could until it arrived; then they were married.

Madame Valmondé had not seen Désirée and the baby for four weeks. When she reached L'Abri she shuddered at the first sight of it, as she always did. It was a sad looking place, which for many years had not known the gentle presence of a mistress, old Monsieur Aubigny having married and buried his wife in France, and she having loved her own land too well ever to leave it. The roof came down steep black like a cowl, reaching out beyond the wide galleries that encircled the yellow stuccoed house. Big, solemn oaks grew close to it, and their thick-leaved, far-reaching branches shadowed it like a pall. Young Aubigny's rule was a strict one, too, and under it his negroes had forgotten how to be gay, as they had been during the old master's easy-going and indulgent lifetime.

The young mother was recovering slowly, and lay full length, in her soft white muslins and laces, upon a couch. The baby was beside her, upon her arm, where he had fallen asleep, at her breast. The yellow nurse woman sat beside a window fanning herself.

Madame Valmondé bent her portly figure over Désirée and kissed her, holding her an instant tenderly in her arms. Then she turned to the child.

'This is not the baby!' she exclaimed, in startled tones. French was the language spoken at Valmondé in those days.

'I knew you would be astonished,' laughed Désirée, 'at the way he has grown. The little *cochon de lait!* Look at his legs, mamma, and his hands and fingernails — real fingernails. Zandrine had to cut them this morning. Isn't it true, Zandrine?'

The woman bowed her turbaned head majestically, 'Mais si, Madame.'

'And the way he cries,' went on Désirée, 'is deafening. Armand heard him the other day as far away as La Blanche's cabin.'

Madame Valmondé had never removed her eyes from the child. She lifted it and walked with it over to the window that was lightest. She scanned the baby narrowly, then looked as searchingly at Zandrine, whose face was turned to gaze across the fields.

'Yes, the child has grown, has changed,' said Madame Valmondé, slowly, as she replaced it beside its mother. 'What does Armand say?'

Désirée's face became suffused with a glow that was happiness itself.

'Oh, Armand is the proudest father in the parish, I believe, chiefly because it is a boy, to bear his name; though he says not, — that he would have loved a girl as well. But I know it isn't true. I know he says that to please me. And mamma,' she added, drawing Madame Valmondé's head down to her, and speaking in a whisper, 'he hasn't punished one of them — not one of them since baby is born. Even Négrillon, who pretended to have burnt his leg that he might rest from work — he only laughed, and said Négrillon was a great scamp. Oh, mamma, I'm so happy; it frightens me.'

What Désirée said was true. Marriage, and later the birth of his son had softened Armand Aubigny's imperious and exacting nature greatly. This was what made the gentle Désirée so happy, for she loved him desperately. When he frowned she trembled, but loved him. When he smiled, she asked no greater blessing of God. But Armand's dark, handsome face had not often been disfigured by frowns since the day he fell in love with her.

When the baby was about three months old, Désirée awoke one day to the convinction that there was something in the air menacing her peace. It was at first too subtle to grasp. It had only been a disquieting suggestion; an air of mystery among the blacks; unexpected visits from far-off neighbours who could hardly account for their coming. Then a strange, an awful change in her husband's manner, which she dared not ask him to explain. When he spoke to her, it was with averted eyes, from which the old love-light seemed to have gone out. He absented himself from home; and when there, avoided her presence and that of her child, without excuse. And the very spirit of Satan seemed suddenly to take hold of him in his dealings with the slaves. Désirée was miserable enough to die.

She sat in her room, one hot afternoon, in her *peignoir*, listlessly drawing through her fingers the strands of her long, silky brown hair that hung about her shoulders. The baby, half naked, lay asleep upon her own great mahogany bed, that was like a sumptuous throne, with its satin-lined half-canopy. One of La Blanche's little quadroon boys — half naked too — stood fanning the child slowly with a fan of peacock feathers. Désirée's eyes had been fixed absently and sadly upon the baby, while she was striving to penetrate the threatening mist that she felt closing about her. She looked from her child to the boy who stood beside him, and back again; over and over. 'Ah!' It was a cry that she could not help; which she was not conscious of having uttered. The blood turned like ice in her veins, and a clammy moisture gathered upon her face.

She tried to speak to the little quadroon boy; but no sound would come, at first. When he heard his name uttered, he looked up, and his mistress was pointing to the door. He laid aside the great, soft fan, and obediently stole away, over the polished floor, on his bare tiptoes.

She stayed motionless, with gaze riveted upon her child, and her face the picture of fright.

Presently her husband entered the room, and without noticing her, went to a table and began to search among some papers which covered it.

'Armand,' she called to him, in a voice which must have stabbed him, if he was human. But he did not notice. 'Armand,' she said again. Then she rose and tottered towards him. 'Armand,' she panted once more, clutching his arm, 'look at our child. What does it mean? Tell me.'

He coldly but gently loosened her fingers from about his arm and thrust the hand away from his. 'Tell me what it means!' she cried despairingly.

'It means,' he answered lightly, 'that the child is not white; it means that you are not white.'

A quick conception of all that this accusation meant for her nerved her with unwonted courage to deny it. 'It's a lie; it is not true, I am white! Look at my hair, it is brown; and my eyes are gray, Armand, you know they are gray. And my skin is fair,' seizing his wrist. 'Look at my hand; whiter than yours, Armand,' she laughed hysterically.

'As white as La Blanche's' he returned cruelly; and went away leaving her alone with their child.

When she could hold a pen in her hand, she sent a despairing letter to Madame Valmondé.

'My mother, they tell me I am not white. Armand has told me I am not white. For God's sake tell them it is not true. You must know it is not true. I shall die. I must die. I cannot be so unhappy, and live.'

The answer that came was as brief:

'My own Désirée: Come home to Valmondé; back to your mother who loves you. Come with your child.'

When the letter reached Désirée she went with it to her husband's study, and laid it open upon the desk before which he sat. She was like a stone image: silent, white, motionless after she placed it there.

In silence he ran his cold eyes over the written words. He said nothing. 'Shall I go, Armand?' she asked in tones sharp with agonised suspense.

'Yes, go.'

'Do you want me to go?'

'Yes, I want you to go.'

He thought Almighty God had dealt cruelly and unjustly with him; and felt, somehow, that he was paying Him back in kind when he stabbed thus into his wife's soul. Moreover he no longer loved her, because of the unconscious injury she had brought upon his home and his name.

She turned away like one stunned by a blow, and walked slowly towards the door, hoping he would call her back.

'Good-bye, Armand,' she moaned.

He did not answer her. That was his last blow at fate.

Désirée went in search of her child. Zandrine was pacing the sombre gallery with it. She took the little one from the nurse's arms with no word of explanation, and descending the steps, walked away, under the live-oak branches.

It was an October afternoon; the sun was just sinking. Out in the still fields the negroes were picking cotton.

Désirée had not changed the thin white garment nor the slippers which she wore. Her hair was uncovered and the sun's rays brought a golden gleam from its brown meshes. She did not take the broad, beaten road which led to the far-off plantation of Valmondé. She walked across a deserted field, where the stubble bruised her tender feet, so delicately shod, and tore her thin gown to shreds.

She disappeared among the reeds and willows that grew thick along the banks of the deep, sluggish bayou; and she did not come back again.

Some weeks later there was a curious scene enacted at L'Abri. In the centre of the smoothly swept back yard was a great bonfire. Armand Aubigny sat in the wide hallway that commanded a view of the spectacle; and it was he who dealt out to a half dozen negroes the material which kept this fire ablaze.

A graceful cradle of willow, with all its dainty furbishings, was laid upon the pyre, which had already been fed with the richness of a priceless *layette*. Then there were silk gowns, and velvet and satin ones added to these; laces, too, and embroideries; bonnets and gloves; for the *corbeille* had been of rare quality.

The last thing to go was a tiny bundle of letters; innocent little scribblings that Désirée had sent to him during the days of their espousal. There was the remnant of one back in the drawer from which he took them. But it was not Désirée; it was part of an old letter from his mother to his father. He read it. She was thanking God for the blessing of her husband's love:—

'But, above all,' she wrote, 'night and day, I thank the good God for having so arranged our lives that our dear Armand will never know that his mother, who adores him, belongs to the race that is cursed with the brand of slavery.'

ROALD DAHL

The Landlady

Billy Weaver had travelled down from London on the slow afternoon train, with a change at Swindon on the way, and by the time he got to Bath it was about 9 o'clock in the evening and the moon was coming up out of a clear starry sky over the houses opposite the station entrance. But the air was deadly cold and the wind was like a flat blade of ice on his cheeks.

'Excuse me,' he said, 'but is there a fairly cheap hotel not too far away from here?'

'Try The Bell and Dragon,' the porter answered, pointing down the road. 'They might take you in. It's about a quarter of a mile along on the other side.'

Billy thanked him and picked up his suitcase and set out to walk the quarter-mile to The Bell and Dragon. He had never been to Bath before. He didn't know anyone who lived there. But Mr Greenslade at the Head Office in London had told him it was a splendid city. 'Find your own lodgings,' he had said, 'and then go along and report to the Branch Manager as soon as you've got yourself settled.'

Billy was seventeen years old. He was wearing a new navy-blue overcoat, a new brown trilby hat, and a new brown suit, and he was feeling fine. He walked briskly down the street. He was trying to do everything briskly these days. Briskness, he had decided, was *the* one common characteristic of all successful

businessmen. The big shots up at Head Office were absolutely
fantastically brisk all the time. They were amazing.

There were no shops on this wide street that he was walking
along, only a line of tall houses on each side, all of them
identical. They had porches and pillars and four or five steps
going up to their front doors, and it was obvious that once upon
a time they had been very swanky residences. But now, even in
the darkness, he could see that the paint was peeling from the
woodwork on their doors and windows, and that the handsome
white façades were cracked and blotchy from neglect.

Suddenly, in a downstairs window that was brilliantly il-
luminated by a street-lamp not six yards away, Billy caught
sight of a printed notice propped up against the glass in one of
the upper panes. It said BED AND BREAKFAST. There was a vase
of pussy willows, tall and beautiful, standing just underneath
the notice.

He stopped walking. He moved a bit closer. Green curtains
(some sort of velvety material) were hanging down on either
side of the window. The pussy willows looked wonderful beside
them. He went right up and peered through the glass into the
room, and the first thing he saw was a bright fire burning in the
hearth. On the carpet in front of the fire, a pretty little dachshund
was curled up asleep with its nose tucked into its belly. The
room itself, so far as he could see in the half-darkness, was filled
with pleasant furniture. There was a baby-grand piano and a
big sofa and several plump armchairs; and in one corner he
spotted a large parrot in a cage. Animals were usually a good
sign in a place like this, Billy told himself; and all in all, it
looked to him as though it would be a pretty decent house to
stay in. Certainly it would be more comfortable than The Bell
and Dragon.

On the other hand, a pub would be more congenial than a
boarding-house. There would be beer and darts in the evenings,
and lots of people to talk to, and it would probably be a good
bit cheaper, too. He had stayed a couple of nights in a pub once
before and he had liked it. He had never stayed in any boarding-
houses, and, to be perfectly honest, he was a tiny bit frightened
of them. The name itself conjured up images of watery cabbage,
rapacious landladies, and a powerful smell of kippers in the
living-room.

After dithering about like this in the cold for two or three minutes. Billy decided that he would walk on and take a look at The Bell and Dragon before making up his mind. He turned to go.

And now a queer thing happened to him. He was in the act of stepping back and turning away from the window when all at once his eye was caught and held in the most peculiar manner by the small notice that was there. BED AND BREAKFAST, it said. BED AND BREAKFAST, BED AND BREAKFAST, BED AND BREAK-FAST. Each word was like a large black eye staring at him through the glass, holding him, compelling him, forcing him to stay where he was and not to walk away from that house, and the next thing he knew, he was actually moving across from the window to the front door of the house, climbing the steps that led up to it, and reaching for the bell.

He pressed the bell. Far away in a back room he heard it ringing, and then *at once* — it must have been at once because he hadn't even had time to take his finger from the bell-button — the door swung open and a woman was standing there.

Normally you ring the bell and you have at least a half-minute's wait before the door opens. But this dame was like a jack-in-the-box. He pressed the bell — and out she popped! It made him jump.

She was about forty-five or fifty years old, and the moment she saw him, she gave him a warm welcoming smile.

'*Please* come in,' she said pleasantly. She stepped aside, holding the door wide open, and Billy found himself automatically starting forward into the house. The compulsion or, more accurately, the desire to follow after her into that house was extraordinarily strong.

'I saw the notice in the window,' he said, holding himself back.

'Yes, I know.'

'I was wondering about a room.'

'It's *all* ready for you, my dear,' she said. She had a round pink face and very gentle blue eyes.

'I was on my way to The Bell and Dragon,' Billy told her. 'But the notice in your window just happened to catch my eye.'

'My dear boy,' she said, 'why don't you come in out of the cold?'

'How much do you charge?'

'Five and sixpence a night, including breakfast.'

It was fantastically cheap. It was less than half of what he had been willing to pay.

'If that is too much,' she added, 'then perhaps I can reduce it just a tiny bit. Do you desire an egg for breakfast? Eggs are expensive at the moment. It would be sixpence less without the egg.'

'Five and sixpence is fine,' he answered. 'I should like very much to stay here.'

'I knew you would. Do come in.'

She seemed terribly nice. She looked exactly like the mother of one's best school-friend welcoming one into the house to stay for the Christmas holidays. Billy took off his hat, and stepped over the threshold.

'Just hang it there,' she said, 'and let me help you with your coat.'

There were no other hats or coats in the hall. There were no umbrellas, no walking-sticks — nothing.

'We have it *all* to ourselves,' she said, smiling at him over her shoulder as she led the way upstairs. 'You see, it isn't very often I have the pleasure of taking a visitor into my little nest.'

The old girl is slightly dotty, Billy told himself. But at five and sixpence a night, who gives a damn about that? 'I should've thought you'd be simply swamped with applicants,' he said politely.

'Oh, I am, my dear, I am, of course I am. But the trouble is that I'm inclined to be just a teeny weeny bit choosy and particular — if you see what I mean.'

'Ah, yes.'

'But I'm always ready. Everything is always ready day and night in the house just on the off-chance that an acceptable young gentleman will come along. And it is such a pleasure, my dear, such a very great pleasure when now and again I open the door and I see someone standing there who is just *exactly* right.' She was half-way up the stairs, and she paused with one hand on the stair-rail, turning her head and smiling down at him with pale lips. 'Like you,' she added, and her blue eyes travelled slowly all the way down the length of Billy's body, to his feet, and then up again.

On the first-floor landing she said to him, 'This floor is mine.'

They climbed up a second flight. 'And this one is *all* yours,' she said. 'Here's your room. I do hope you'll like it.' She took him into a small but charming front bedroom, switching on the light as she went in.

'The morning sun comes right in the window, Mr Perkins. It *is* Mr Perkins, isn't it?'

'No,' he said. 'It's Weaver.'

'Mr Weaver. How nice. I've put a water-bottle between the sheets to air them out, Mr Weaver. It's such a comfort to have a hot water-bottle in a strange bed with clean sheets, don't you agree? And you may light the gas fire at any time if you feel chilly.'

'Thank you,' Billy said. 'Thank you ever so much.' He noticed that the bedspread had been taken off the bed, and that the bedclothes had been neatly turned back on one side, all ready for someone to get in.

'I'm so glad you appeared,' she said, looking earnestly into his face. 'I was beginning to get worried.'

'That's all right,' Billy answered brightly. 'You mustn't worry about me.' He put his suitcase on the chair and started to open it.

'And what about supper, my dear? Did you manage to get anything to eat before you came here?'

'I'm not a bit hungry, thank you,' he said. 'I think I'll just go to bed as soon as possible because tomorrow I've got to get up rather early and report to the office.'

'Very well, then. I'll leave you now so that you can unpack. But before you go to bed, would you be kind enough to pop into the sitting-room on the ground floor and sign the book? Everyone has to do that because it's the law of the land, and we don't want to go breaking any laws at *this* stage in the proceedings, do we?' She gave him a little wave of the hand and went quickly out of the room and closed the door.

Now, the fact that his landlady appeared to be slightly off her rocker didn't worry Billy in the least. After all, she was not only harmless — there was no question about that — but she was also quite obviously a kind and generous soul. He guessed that she had probably lost a son in the war, or something like that, and had never got over it.

So a few minutes later, after unpacking his suitcase and washing his hands, he trotted downstairs to the ground floor and entered the living-room. His landlady wasn't there, but the fire was glowing in the hearth, and the little dachshund was still sleeping in front of it. The room was wonderfully warm and cosy. I'm a lucky fellow, he thought, rubbing his hands. This is a bit of all right.

He found the guest-book lying open on the piano, so he took out his pen and wrote down his name and address. There were only two other entries above his on the page, and, as one always does with guest-books, he started to read them. One was a Christopher Mulholland from Cardiff. The other was Gregory W. Temple from Bristol.

That's funny, he thought suddenly. Christopher Mulholland. It rings a bell.

Now where on earth had he heard that rather unusual name before?

Was he a boy at school? No. Was it one of his sister's numerous young men, perhaps, or a friend of his father's? No, no, it wasn't any of those. He glanced down again at the book.

Christopher Mulholland   231 Cathedral Road, Cardiff
Gregory W. Temple   27 Sycamore Drive, Bristol

As a matter of fact, now he came to think of it, he wasn't at all sure that the second name didn't have almost as much of a familiar ring about it as the first.

'Gregory Temple?' he said aloud, searching his memory. 'Christopher Mulholland? . . .'

'Such charming boys,' a voice behind him answered, and he turned and saw his landlady sailing into the room with a large silver tea-tray in her hands. She was holding it well out in front of her, and rather high up, as though the tray were a pair of reins on a frisky horse.

'They sound somehow familiar,' he said.

'They do? How interesting.'

'I'm almost positive I've heard those names before somewhere. Isn't that queer? Maybe it was in the newspapers. They weren't famous in any way, were they? I mean famous cricketers or footballers or something like that?'

'Famous,' she said, setting the tea-tray down on the low table in front of the sofa. 'Oh no, I don't think they were famous. But they were extraordinarily handsome, both of them, I can promise you that. They were tall and young and handsome, my dear, just exactly like you.'

Once more, Billy glanced down at the book. 'Look here,' he said, noticing the dates. 'This last entry is over two years old.'

'It is?'

'Yes, indeed. And Christopher Mulholland's is nearly a year before that — more than *three years ago*.'

'Dear me,' she said, shaking her head and heaving a dainty little sigh. 'I would never have thought it. How time does fly away from us all, doesn't it, Mr Wilkins?'

'It's Weaver,' Billy said. 'W-e-a-v-e-r.'

'Oh, of course it is?' she cried, sitting down on the sofa. 'How silly of me. I do apologise. In one ear and out the other, that's me, Mr Weaver.'

'You know something?' Billy said. 'Something that's really quite extraordinary about all this?'

'No, dear, I don't.'

'Well, you see — both of these names, Mulholland and Temple, I not only seem to remember each one of them separately, so to speak, but somehow or other, in some peculiar way, they both appear to be sort of connected together as well. As though they were both famous for the same sort of thing, if you see what I mean — like . . . well . . . like Dempsey and Tunney, for example, or Churchill and Roosevelt.'

'How amusing,' she said. 'But come over here now, dear, and sit down beside me on the sofa and I'll give you a nice cup of tea and a ginger biscuit before you go to bed.'

'You really shouldn't bother,' Billy said. 'I didn't mean you to do anything like that.' He stood by the piano, watching her as she fussed about with the cups and saucers. He noticed that she had small, white, quickly moving hands, and red fingernails.

'I'm almost positive it was in the newspapers I saw them,' Billy said. 'I'll think of it in a second. I'm sure I will.'

There is nothing more tantalising than a thing like this which lingers just outside the borders of one's memory. He hated to give up.

'Now wait a minute,' he said. 'Wait just a minute. Mul-holland . . . Christopher Mulholland . . . wasn't *that* the name of the Eton schoolboy who was on a walking-tour through the West Country, and then all of a sudden . . .'

'Milk?' she said. 'And sugar?'

'Yes, please. And then all of a sudden . . .'

'Eton schoolboy?' she said, 'Oh no, my dear, that can't possibly be right because *my* Mr Mulholland was certainly not an Eton schoolboy when he came to me. He was a Cambridge under-graduate. Come over here now and sit next to me and warm yourself in front of this lovely fire. Come on. Your tea's all ready for you.' She patted the empty place beside her on the sofa, and she sat there smiling at Billy and waiting for him to come over.

He crossed the room slowly, and sat down on the edge of the sofa. She placed his teacup on the table in front of him.

'*There* we are,' she said. 'How nice and cosy this is, isn't it?'

Billy started sipping his tea. She did the same. For half a minute or so, neither of them spoke. But Billy knew that she was looking at him. Her body was half-turned towards him and he could feel her eyes resting on his face, watching him over the rim of her teacup. Now and again, he caught a whiff of a peculiar smell that seemed to emanate directly from her person. It was not in the least unpleasant, and it reminded him — well, he wasn't quite sure what it reminded him of. Pickled walnuts? New leather? Or was it the corridors of a hospital?

'Mr Mulholland was a great one for his tea,' she said at length. 'Never in my life have I seen anyone drink as much tea as dear, sweet Mr Mulholland.'

'I suppose he left fairly recently,' Billy said. He was positive now that he had seen them in the newspapers — in the headlines.

'Left?' she said, arching her brows. 'But my dear boy, he never left. He's still here. Mr Temple is also here. They're on the third floor, both of them together.'

Billy set down his cup slowly on the table, and stared at his landlady. She smiled back at him, and then she put out one of her white hands and patted him comfortingly on the knee.

'How old are you, my dear?' she asked.

'Seventeen.'

'Seventeen!' she cried. 'Oh, it's the perfect age! Mr Mulholland was also seventeen. But I think he was a trifle shorter than you are, in fact I'm sure he was, and his teeth weren't *quite* so white. You have the most beautiful teeth, Mr Weaver, did you know that?'

'They're not as good as they look,' Billy said. 'They've got simply masses of fillings in them at the back.'

'Mr Temple, of course, was a little older,' she said, ignoring his remark. 'He was actually twenty-eight. And yet I never would have guessed it if he hadn't told me, never in my whole life. There wasn't a *blemish* on his body.'

'A what?' Billy said.

'His skin was *just* like a baby's.'

There was a pause. Billy picked up his teacup and took another sip of his tea, then he set it down again gently in its saucer. He waited for her to say something else, but she seemed to have lapsed into another of her silences. He sat there staring ahead of him into the far corner of the room, biting his lower lip.

'That parrot,' he said at last. 'You know something? It had me completely fooled when I first saw it through the window from the street. I could have sworn it was alive.'

'Alas, no longer.'

'It's most terribly clever the way it's been done,' he said. 'It doesn't look in the least bit dead. Who did it?'

'I did.'

'*You* did?'

'Of course,' she said. 'And have you met my little Basil as well?' She nodded towards the dachshund curled up so comfortably in front of the fire. Billy looked at it. And suddenly, he realised that this animal had all the time been just as silent and motionless as the parrot. He put out a hand and touched it gently on the top of its back. The back was hard and cold, and when he pushed the hair to one side with his fingers, he could see the skin underneath, greyish-black and dry and perfectly preserved.

'Good gracious me,' he said. 'How absolutely fascinating.' He turned away from the dog and stared with deep admiration at the little woman beside him on the sofa. 'It must be most awfully difficult to do a thing like that.'

'Not in the least,' she said. 'I stuff *all* my little pets myself when they pass away. Will you have another cup of tea?'

'No, thank you,' Billy said. The tea tasted faintly of bitter almonds, and he didn't much care for it.

'You did sign the book, didn't you?'

'Oh, yes.'

'That's good. Because later on, if I happen to forget what you were called, then I can always come down here and look it up. I still do that almost every day with Mr Mulholland and Mr . . . Mr . . .'

'Temple,' Billy said. 'Gregory Temple. Excuse me asking, but haven't there been *any* other guests here except them in the last two or three years?'

Holding her teacup high in one hand, inclining her head slightly to the left, she looked up at him out of the corners of her eyes and gave him another gentle little smile.

'No, my dear,' she said. 'Only you.'

GUY DE MAUPASSANT

Vendetta

Paolo Saverini's widow dwelt alone with her son in a small, mean house on the ramparts of Bonifacio. Built on a spur of the mountain and in places actually overhanging the sea, the town looks across the rockstrewn straits to the low-lying coast of Sardinia. On the other side, girdling it almost completely, there is a fissure in the cliff, like an immense corridor, which serves as a port, and down this long channel, as far as the first houses, sail the small Italian and Sardinian fishing boats, and once a fortnight the broken-winded old steamer from Ajaccio. Clustered together on the white hill-side, the houses form a patch of even more dazzling whiteness. Clinging to the rock, gazing down upon those deadly straits where scarcely a ship ventures, they look like the nests of birds of prey. The sea and the barren coast, stripped of all but a scanty covering of grass, are for ever harassed by a restless wind, which sweeps along the narrow funnel, ravaging the banks on either side. In all directions the black points of innumerable rocks jut out from the water, with trails of white foam streaming from them, like torn shreds of linen, floating and fluttering on the surface of the waves.

The widow Saverini's house was planted on the very edge of the cliff, and its three windows opened upon this wild and dreary prospect. She lived there with her son Antoine and their dog Sémillante, a great gaunt brute of the sheep-dog variety,

47

with a long, rough coat, which the young man took with him when he went out shooting.

One evening, after a quarrel, Antoine Saverini was treacherously stabbed by Nicolas Ravolati, who escaped that same night to Sardinia.

At the sight of the body, which was brought home by passersby, the old mother shed no tears, but she gazed long and silently at her dead son. Then, laying her wrinkled hand upon the corpse, she promised him the vendetta. She would not allow any one to remain with her, and shut herself up with the dead body. The dog Sémillante, who remained with her, stood at the foot of the bed and howled, with her head stretched out towards her master and her tail between her legs. Neither of them stirred, neither the dog nor the old mother, who was now leaning over the body, gazing at it fixedly, and silently shedding great tears. Still wearing his rough jacket, which was pierced and torn at the breast, the boy lay on his back as if asleep, but there was blood all about him, on his shirt, which had been stripped off in order to expose the wound, on his waistcoat and his trousers, face and hands. His beard and hair were matted with clots of blood.

The old mother began to talk to him, and at the sound of her voice the dog stopped howling.

'Never fear, never fear, you shall be avenged, my son, my little son, my poor child. You may sleep in peace. You shall be avenged, I tell you. You have your mother's word, and you know she never breaks it.'

Slowly she bent down and pressed her cold lips to the dead lips of her son.

Sémillante resumed her howling, uttering a monotonous, long-drawn wail, heart-rending and terrible. And thus the two remained, the woman and the dog, till morning.

The next day Antoine Saverini was buried, and soon his name ceased to be mentioned in Bonifacio.

He had no brother, nor any near male relation. There was no man in the family who could take up the vendetta. Only his mother, his old mother, brooded over it.

From morning till night she could see, just across the straits, a white speck upon the coast. This was the little Sardinian village of Longosardo, where the Corsican bandits took refuge whenever the hunt for them grew too hot. They formed almost the entire population of the hamlet. In full view of their native shores they waited for a chance to return home and take to the 'maquis' again. She knew that Nicolas Ravolati had sought shelter in that village.

All day long she sat alone at her window gazing at the opposite coast and thinking of her revenge, but what was she to do with no one to help her, and she herself so feeble and near her end? But she had promised; she had sworn by the dead body of her son; she could not forget, and she dared not delay. What was she to do? She could not sleep at night, she knew not a moment of rest or peace, but racked her brains unceasingly. Sémillante, asleep at her feet, would now and then raise her head and emit a piercing howl. Since her master had disappeared, this had become a habit; it was as if she were calling him, as if she, too, were inconsolable and preserved in her canine soul an indelible memory of the dead.

One night, when Sémillante began to whine, the old mother had an inspiration of savage, vindictive ferocity. She thought about it till morning. At daybreak she rose and went to church. Kneeling on the stone floor, humbling herself before God, she begged Him to aid and support her, to lend to her poor, worn-out body the strength she needed to avenge her son.

Then she returned home. In the yard stood an old barrel with one end knocked in, which caught the rainwater from the eaves. She turned it over, emptied it, and fixed it to the ground with stakes and stones. Then she chained up Sémillante to this kennel and went into the house.

With her eyes fixed on the Sardinian coast, she walked restlessly up and down her room. He was over there, the murderer.

The dog howled all day and night. The next morning the old woman brought her a bowl of water, but no food, neither soup nor bread. Another day passed. Sémillante was worn out and slept. The next morning her eyes were gleaming, and her coat dulled, and she tugged frantically at her chain. And again the old woman gave her nothing to eat. Maddened with hunger Sémillante barked hoarsely. Another night went by.

At daybreak, the widow went to a neighbour and begged for two trusses of straw. She took some old clothes that had belonged to her husband, stuffed them with straw to represent a human figure, and made a head out of a bundle of old rags. Then, in front of Sémillante's kennel, she fixed a stake in the ground and fastened the dummy to it in an upright position.

The dog looked at the straw figure in surprise and, although she was famished, stopped howling.

The old woman went to the pork butcher and bought a long piece of black blood pudding. When she came home she lit a wood fire in the yard, close to the kennel, and fried the black pudding. Sémillante bounded up and down in a frenzy, foaming at the mouth, her eyes fixed on the pan with its maddening smell of meat.

Her mistress took the steaming pudding and wound it like a cravat round the dummy's neck. She fastened it on tightly with string as if to force it inwards. When she had finished, she unchained the dog.

With one ferocious leap, Sémillante flew at the dummy's throat and, with her paws on its shoulders, began to tear it. She fell back with a portion of her prey between her jaws, sprang at it again, slashing at the string with her fangs, tore away some scraps of food, dropped for a moment, and hurled herself at it in renewed fury. She tore away the whole face and reduced the neck to shreds.

Motionless and silent, with burning eyes, the old woman looked on. Presently she chained the dog up again. She starved her another two days, and then put her through the same strange performance. For three months she accustomed her to this method of attack, and to tear her meals away with her fangs. She was no longer kept on the chain. At a sign from her mistress, the dog would fly at the dummy's throat.

She learned to tear it to pieces even when no food was concealed about its throat. Afterwards as a reward she was always given the black pudding her mistress had cooked for her.

As soon as she caught sight of the dummy, Sémillante quivered with excitement and looked at her mistress, who would raise her finger and cry in a shrill voice, 'Tear him!'

One Sunday morning when she thought the time had come, the widow Saverini went to confession and communion, in an ecstasy of devotion. Then she disguised herself like a tattered old beggar man, and struck a bargain with a Sardinian fisherman, who took her and her dog across to the opposite shore.

She carried a large piece of black pudding wrapped in a cloth bag. Sémillante had been starved for two days, and her mistress kept exciting her by letting her smell the savoury food.

The pair entered the village of Longosardo. The old woman hobbled along to a baker and asked for the house of Nicolas Ravolati. He had resumed his former occupation, which was that of a joiner, and he was working alone in the back of his shop.

The old woman threw open the door and called:

'Nicolas! Nicolas!'

He turned round. Slipping the dog's lead, she cried:

'Tear him! Tear him!'

The maddened animal flew at his throat. The man flung out his arms and grappled with the brute, and they rolled on the ground together. For some moments he struggled, kicking the floor with his feet. Then he lay still, while Sémillante tore his throat to shreds.

Two neighbours, seated at their doors, remembered seeing an old beggar man emerge from the house and, at his heels, a lean black dog, which was eating, as it went along, some brown substance that its master was giving it.

By the evening the old woman had reached home again.

That night she slept well.

MARJORIE DARKE

The Birthday Present

'Mashed, that's what,' old Fatty Scrimshaw said. 'Mashed to a pulp. I tell you there was hardly a brick left standing.'

Old Fatty lives on the same landing as us in the Tower Block and he's always popping in for a chat. Which means gabbing on for hours and hours about the war. Now I don't mind hearing about how the Jerry bombers came zooming over . . . eeeooow eeeooow like that — dropping their load of incendiaries on the middle of our town, and about how you could see the flames as far away as Leicester. Or even about Mrs Fatty running out in her dinky curlers and second best nightie, losing a slipper on the way and yowling louder than a dog when its tail gets trodden on — but not when I've heard it forty-five million times before! It's enough to make your ears drop off.

He was on about it now. Jabbing with his finger at the Marley tiles on our floor.

'Right here where I'm standing. Thirty-eight years to the day it was. A whole row of houses. You know — the kind with the weaver's top-shops. Real nice places and built to last. That's a laugh if you like! Gone in less time than it takes to tell you now, Mrs Hollins.' He wheezed out this gusty sigh and nodded at our Mam.

Mostly when he does that I like to watch because his three chins wobble and he screws up his eyes as the wobble runs up

his cheeks, just as if they're made of jelly. He scratches his bald
head too, and leaves red marks like railway tracks. But today I
wasn't interested. All I wanted was to get out.

'Go on!' Mam roared, because he's deaf as six wads of
chewing-gum. Sometimes I think she's quite loony, the things
she lets herself in for. But she just says he's lonely, and a bit of
time is worth more than a ten-pound note.

'True as the sun rises,' old Fatty said, warming to it. 'On this
very spot was where O'Malley lived with his missus and a raft
of kids. They were a lively lot, I'll tell you! My stars . . . the
things them lads used to get up to. Tricks? Like a cartload of
monkeys they were!' He paused and chuckled — remembering.
Then he went on: 'Oh yes . . and over there, more or less under
your Kevin's bedroom, was the Dreefes. Mister and his missus
and . . .'

I stopped listening and tried to figure out just how I was going
to get away from our flat. He was standing right in front of the
door, practically sitting on the handle. I measured the space by
eye, but it was hopeless. As he's as big as a tractor there was *no
way*! If I was to say 'Excuse me', I'd have to yell and then our
Mam would want to know where I thought I was going at that
time of a Saturday night when our team had been playing
Spurs . . . and didn't I ever take a blind bit of notice what she
said? You see she's okay about most things, but nutty as nine
fruitcakes when it comes to soccer matches and Hooligans —
her name for anyone who goes to watch. I've tried telling her
she's got it all wrong, but you might as well try pushing a bus
over. Not that I'm bonkers about soccer like our Dave. I don't
want to see Spurs give us a roasting! But I do *hate* being stuck
five floors up on a Saturday, with nothing on telly except some
crummy film, and my skateboard screaming at me to come and
whizz about on it. And that's another thing our Mam doesn't
approve of — skateboards. 'Old Lady Killers' she calls them.
She didn't half shred our Dave when he gave me one for my
birthday.

'A birthday on the thirteenth and you give him a *skateboard*!'
She said in a voice that could've skewered a centipede at long
range.

At the time I bristled. Couldn't she see how beautiful it was?

All green and silver and strong as a Jumbo Jet. It wouldn't snap at the first bit of stress. I wanted to explain that it was perfectly safe, but knew it was useless. When our Mam gets started, the only thing to do is let her talk till she's tired. So I did.

After, I went for my first fantastic skate. I didn't fall off either. Our Mam looked as if she'd expected me to come home a mangled wreck. But she didn't say so. The talking was over — for the moment!

Now I looked desperately at old Fatty. He'd just got to the bit about coming out of the air-raid shelter next morning and finding Mrs F's unmentionables (his word for her knickers) drooping over a gas-lamp.

'Fancy that, Kevin,' he said, clamping his hand on my shoulder.

I groaned inside. Blazing saddles . . . I hadn't a hope! And then our Mam of all people, came to the rescue.

'Come into the kitchen, Mr Scrimshaw,' she bellowed. 'Sit down and rest your legs. I'll make us a nice cuppa.'

I didn't waste any more time. Reckoning that the tea-making would take about five minutes, I pulled my skateboard from behind our Dave's old cardboard box, where he keeps his motorbike spares, buzzed out of the flat and was three flights down before I heard Mam calling:

'Kev . . . Ke*vin*!'

I kept going. It would mean a belting when I got back, but it was worth it. There were two routes to the place where I was heading. The long way is all streets, but there's a short cut through the cemetery. It's a bit weird when it gets dark. Orange light from the naphtha lamps on the main road, drips through the trees and makes these spidery shapes which grab at you when the wind gets up. There was a stiff breeze now, but I risked it. After all I'd had to hang about long enough already. By this time it was getting pretty dark and the gravestones stood up like giants' mossy teeth — huge and gappy. The breeze made the trees dip and scratch with knotted twig fingers. They aren't too well looked after — the trees I mean — and they hang down low. So you can imagine what I felt like when one combed my hair for me! I did this Olympic jump about six miles high. There was a smell too. I tried to think what it reminded me of, but was in too much of a tearing rush to work it out. I was glad to get

shot of the place and reach the jetty, I can tell you! Gave me the
creeps it did.

Galloping across the waste ground at the end of the jetty, I
arrived at the main road which circles our town. Part of this
road is up on stilts with other roads crossing beneath. There's a
subway tunnel as well, for people on foot. It forks at the far end
— left to the station and right to Jakes Road. Skateboarding
isn't allowed, but lots of kids do. It's okay so long as you keep
your eyes peeled for nosy parkers who'll tell on you.

It was really dark when I got there. A queer purplish sort of
gloom that reached towards the subway, but got cut off by the
bright strip lighting. I could hear traffic zooming along the main
road. The usual weekend stream of cars making for the pubs.
One or two people in their Saturday gear were walking through
the subway — no one that mattered. I put my skateboard down.
A couple of left-foot pushes and I was on my way, doing this
knockout slalom loop round a bloke in cowboy boots and a
black velvet suit. Then curving sharp left so as to miss an Indian
woman pushing a pram.

There are moments when you feel as if everything has dropped
together. Balance, timing, confidence . . . the lot. This was one
of those times. All the creepy quakes I'd experienced coming
through the cemetery, vanished. I felt terrific. I *was* terrific, as I
stood, squatted, leaned and snaked from side to side. Fantastic!
But I knew it was going to be seventy million times better
coming back. Picking up my skateboard, I started up the slope.

That's when I first saw him. Up at the top he was. A skinny
bit of a kid, standing on skates that were much too big. They
were a tatty old-fashioned roller pair with steel wheels, and
looked really weird on the end of his matchstick legs. I couldn't
help wondering where he'd found them — at a jumble sale by
the look. His eyes were out on stalks in this pinched-up face as
he watched me. He didn't look a little kid somehow. His face
had a queer sort of old-young look that made it difficult to guess
what age he was. But he wore short trousers — which seemed
odd on such a cold November night. Huge hands he had too.
Hanging off spindly wrists that were sticking out of a sweater
ten miles too short. I must admit I felt a bit narked. He'd better
not get in the way, I thought, putting my board down again. I

was planning this spectacular nose-wheelie sequence and didn't fancy tangling with a shrimp on rollers out of the ark.

Slap slap with my right foot and I was whooshing along. Both feet on now. Doing a ton across the mouth of the tunnel. Timing perfect as I balanced first on four wheels then on two. I was Boy Skateboard Wonder. Olympic Gold Medal variety!

But I wasn't alone. That kid was just behind. For a minute I felt mad. The nit . . . what did he think he was doing? But I couldn't stay furious. If I was terrific, he was out of this world! There was nothing he couldn't do on those mouldy old skates — turns, spins, figures of eight. I tell you I felt quite jealous!

We swooped up towards the station. I grinned in admiration. I just couldn't help it. And he grinned back. Then, without having to say a word, we set off like one man, as if we'd been practising for weeks. Weaving, turning, cutting across each other with split second precision. It was fabulous! Up at the Jakes Road end I stopped to get my breath. He was just behind and I could see him watching me. There was a kind of hungry look in his eyes and I knew exactly what he wanted.

'Like a go?' I asked — casually, so he wouldn't guess I was itching to try his skates.

He nodded and his pinched white face seemed almost to glow.

'Down and back twice then. Give us your skates.'

We did the swop and I started to buckle on the old skates. I was hearing these queer echoing crashing sounds at the same time, like voices and thunder crackling inside seventy-six empty oil drums. I tried shaking my head and the noise dulled down, but didn't go away. It was a bit rattling. To cover up, I fiddled with the skate straps some more, asking him what he was called.

'Stan.'

The name was in my ears. I wasn't looking straight at him (I was still hunched over my feet) but I could've sworn his mouth didn't move. He stroked my skateboard as if it was a favourite pet cat, then put it down and shoved off just as though he'd been doing it all his life.

'Hang on!' I shouted, standing up and staggering like a drunk as I aimed for the subway entrance where he'd been heading.

'Wait for me!' I felt a right nana, I can tell you. Twice I nearly
hit the deck. On my feet his almost magical skates turned into
awkward lumbering booby-traps. I lurched forward a few paces.
Tipped dangerously. Righted myself — only to find he wasn't
there. The noises which had sunk into the background came
back, though. Real noises this time. A bunch of yobs in scarves
and bobble hats, with football favours pinned to their anoraks,
were surging towards me. Most were waving cans of beer. Not
their first by the yodels and ear-splitting catcalls that echoed
through the subway.

Too late I thought of all Mam's blood-curdling Hooligan
tales, as they spotted me and started calling out:

'Here, look what we've found . . .'

'It's Popeye . . .'

'No it ain't . . .'

'Yer it is . . . before he ate his spinach!'

'Give us a go on yer skates, kid . . .'

I wanted to run, but there was no chance with my feet going
in all directions. If I'd had my board I might have escaped. In a
daft sort of way I half turned, looking for some bolt-hole, and
saw Stan at the mouth of the subway. He was on my board —
my beautiful skateboard.

The yobs saw too. 'Gerroff that skateboard, Skinny!'

'Beat it, Stan,' I yelled. 'Scram . . . *quick!*'

The next thing I knew was that one of the yobs had hurled a
can at me which caught my shin and made me hop and curse.
Then, of course, I lost my balance and fell against one of his
mates, who shoved me into one of the others, who shoved me
back . . . It got a bit rougher each time. They were laughing, but
I felt pretty scared. The hairs on the back of my neck prickled,
and a strong yearning to be in front of our telly watching that
crummy film, hit me. Anywhere would be better than here! I
don't know how long they might have gone on tackling and
passing me like a human football, but midway from one to
another I caught sight of something hurtling towards us. Straight
and swift as a bullet it came.

Stan. On my skateboard!

The yobs had seen him as well. They panicked and tried to get
out of the way, but everything was happening too fast and there

was nowhere to go. I couldn't move. It was just as if the old skates had grown roots and were keeping me plonk in the middle of the subway. In spite of all the racket and jostle, I felt as alone as if I'd been standing on the moon. I was picturing the chaos to come. There'd be a heap of sprawling bodies, and underneath . . . shattered wreckage of plastic, wood and steel.

But it didn't happen like that.

One of the yobs lunged out, meaning to grab Stan and pull him off the board, but froze where he stood and the look on his face could've curdled ten gallons of milk!

For Stan travelled through the lot of us. Yes, *through*! Like a power-boat slicing water. Even now I don't know how it happened. All I remember of the actual moment is a terrible icy cold, deafening silence that cut off the world, and this strong nostril-tingling smell of mildewed biscuits. How long it lasted is another mystery. A second? A year? It seemed like both. Then noises came back. Noises made by running feet as the yobs scattered, scared to death, leaving me stunned and really alone.

No. That's not true. I wasn't quite alone. My skateboard was lodged against the wall at the far end of the tunnel. No Stan. No skates either I realised as I began to run towards it.

Scooping up the skateboard I went on running, my feet taking me across the waste ground and through the cemetery. Running . . . running . . . not noticing eerie naphtha light or bony tree fingers or mossy gravestone teeth this time. I had one goal — HOME!

When I got there, old Fatty Scrimshaw was still in the kitchen. He hadn't got off his favourite subject.

'Wiped out,' he was saying. 'Every man jack, would you believe?' He shook his bald head.

Our Mam was nodding, eyes glued to his face as if this was the very first time she'd ever heard the story. Quivery though I still was, I couldn't help marvelling at the way she could act. She deserved an Oscar!

Old Fatty brought out a large checked hanky and blew his nose. 'Every man jack . . . except the youngest Dreefe lad. They never did find him. Mind you, a lot went missing that night. Funny lad he was. Quiet. Thin as a piece of string, with great big hands.'

A queer feeling started under my ears and worked down my neck. Like seventy-eight spiders doing a war dance. There was something I wanted to ask, but the question stuck to my teeth.

'Where'd he gone?' our Mam shouted.

A sigh escaped old Fatty and he shrugged his mountain shoulders. 'Out on them old skates his brother give him of course. You couldn't keep him off 'em. Mind you, nobody saw him go. But I reckon that's what happened. He was really taken with them roller skates. Could've gone on the Halls he was that good.' He leaned towards Mam, and under the kitchen light his eyes showed up damp. 'Time and again he used to go to the top of our street, come whizzing down, turn a figure of eight and stop dead at the front door, neat as you please. I tell you, Mrs Hollins, if I had one of them new-fangled fifty pences for every time I've seen him do that, I'd be a rich man now.'

Our Mam seemed wrapped in the story. She hadn't spotted me. 'He can't just've vanished.'

Old Fatty sighed again. 'There were a lot o' bombs fell that night.'

'You mean they didn't find so much as a hair of his head?'

'Not one. Not even a wheel off his skates.'

All this time I'd been standing still as a goal-post, but he looked away from our Mam and straight at me. Little sparks of light flicked off the damp in his eyes, but he wheezed out a laugh and the wobble ran from his chins into the crinkling skin. 'You don't get skates for your birthday and not use 'em, eh, Kevin?'

Our Mam swivelled round in her chair. She was frowning and I started to quake all over again. I heard her say:

'*Skating* . . .' in her centipede-skewering voice. Then she paused and gave a little snort, staring at me. I saw her grim face relax, and her voice came out sort of croaky: 'You've skated on some pretty thin ice tonight, me lad!' Picking up the biscuit tin, she held it out. She was *almost* smiling.

I took a Jammy Dodger and bit it. The smell was oat-sweet, gooey, biscuity. Then I remembered, and there wasn't any need for my question. That was it — biscuits . . . *mouldy* biscuits. The graveyard smell. I *knew*. The whole story nearly spilled out of me then and there, specially with old Fatty still damp around the eyes. Maybe it would help if I told? But something held me back.

Our Mam got up to put the kettle on again and I slipped into my bedroom, shutting the door.

'That's two I owe you, Stan,' I said, quiet like so no one else would hear. 'Thanks!'

After all, how am I to know when I might need saving again?

Personal Essay
by Marjorie Darke

'Me . . . read short stories? Never! They are so *boring* . . .'

Or so I thought for years, though like many people I was brought up on fairy tales and loved them. Hans Andersen, the brothers Grimm, Perrault, all were short story writers, though are not as a rule considered as such. So, I went on ignoring this area of writing until the switch-on happened. I discovered the amazing O. Henry! He was an American short story writer of outstanding skill. Master of the 'twist in the tail', that clever about turn at the very end of the story, he made it seem so easy. Hooked by these gems of his, I moved on to James Thurber, another American, whose crazy dogs, falling beds and family mayhem, had me aching with laughter. From there a side-step to Katherine Mansfield. Haunting, brilliant, short-lived, but whose immaculate creations of people and relationships will live as long as there is anyone left to read them.

Each of these writers spoke with entirely different story-voices, but they shared one all important thing. They made sure *every word worked hard*. A short story, unlike its more expansive cousin the novel, has no time nor space for lengthy description or a leisurely unfolding of the plot, and usually deals with people and what is happening, on a small scale. One or two characters. A single incident. A brief length of time. Examining everything with the burning intensity of detail you get when looking down a microscope at a spider's leg or droplet of pond life.

As I read I was slowly learning all this, but a more painful truth did not strike me until I began trying to write a short story myself. Rapidly I discovered how treasured sentences, even whole paragraphs sometimes must be ruthlessly cut out. Learning to 'murder your darlings' someone once described this uncomfortable business. Every short story writer, every *writer*, has to face and accept the fact that you can't keep that juicy bit of description or cunning conversation just because it *is* juicy or cunning and you invented and have fallen in love with it! If the words don't fit and do their job of helping the story, then out they must go. The battle to give in and sacrifice these 'darlings' can waste a lot of time as well, I discovered — liking rich description, which may have a place in longer fiction, but can act like great wads of cottonwool, blocking the tight outlines I was after.

The 'voice' — the way a tale is told — is also of high importance to short story and novel writer alike. Setting the atmosphere in just the

right way can make or break any story. Which means that careful
decisions have to be made early on about *how* the story is told. Will it
be racy first-person, which makes the action bowl along but presents a
one-sided view of what is happening? Or would a more all-round
picture be better — the writer letting the story be seen through the eyes
of several people? Choice of words and how they are strung together,
can also have a strong effect, creating mystery, humour, sadness,
boisterous joy, still calm, or mixtures drawn from any of these. Short
sentences can speed up a story that needs to move fast. Though as a
general rule most stories are helped by a fair balance of long and short
sentences, so that the music of the words and the rhythms they make
together when read aloud, is easy on the ear.

Listening is, indeed, a very necessary part of every writer's life.
Listening to the way real people talk — the words they use, pet
phrases, accents. Listening to the characters in the story, because they
too, should talk in an individual way like real people. They must also
behave true to their personalities, which asks for a different kind of
listening. This time to the story-people themselves when they speak
directly to their creator, as they will if pushed along paths they don't
wish to go. Most writers have had the experience of characters taking
over and directing the story. A delicate bond exists between every
writer and the people she/he has conjured out of words. Constant
attention, alertness, *listening* is needed to make sure these new people
are alive and breathing, not just cardboard cut-outs. The reader should
have the feeling that every person, each relationship, all that happens
in the story, is comfortable and could not have been written any other
way. Like a jigsaw, each piece must slot into its own place. No other
position will do.

But none of these things, voice, characters, atmosphere, sentence
construction, choice of words, story music, can be considered before
the foundation stone is laid. Not a single word can be written without
the vital IDEA. Ideas can arrive from anywhere at any time — at a bus
stop, watching TV, from conversation, reading books, newspapers —
but sometimes they seem to take a mean delight in nipping just out of
reach of the sweating writer! The idea for 'The Birthday Present'
played this trick, until one day, walking to town through a complex
subway system where several paths travelled downhill and met, a boy
on a skateboard came sailing past me. His skill was effortless, superb.
As he swooped by, a childhood memory was triggered. Myself,
enviously watching another boy swooping along the pavement on his
new roller-skates which had shining steel wheels. From there it was a
short step to wondering what these two, present day and war-time
boys, would think of each others' skates and skills. It was an even
shorter step into imagining them meeting. In fact they could have met,
but the war-time boy would be middle-aged. I wanted the immediacy
of each *boy* seeing the other, and that could only be through the

medium of a ghost story. Precisely what I wanted to write! What kind of boys were they, I wondered? Why had the war-time boy died young? It could have been an accident, but more likely in this war-torn city it would have been because of an air-raid. In my mind's eye I saw the awful picture of bombs exploding, reducing a row of houses, homes of many families, into heaps of rubble that sprawled across the road. Screaming and thunder of more bombs. Great jets of water from shattered mains, fountained into the air. Then, from beneath a pile of bricks and broken furniture, came a boy. Thin, wearing a tatty version of the splendid metal roller-skates I had envied all those years ago, he seemed unhurt, though was curiously pale.

'Thanks, Stan,' I said.

Why Stan? I don't know. He was always Stan from that moment. Perhaps he had told me.

Who knows?

O. HENRY

The Ransom of Red Chief

It looked like a good thing: but wait till I tell you. We were down South, in Alabama — Bill Driscoll and myself — when this kidnapping idea struck us. It was, as Bill afterward expressed it, 'during a moment of temporary mental apparition'; but we didn't find that out till later.

There was a town down there, as flat as a flannel cake, and called Summit, of course. It contained inhabitants of as undeleterious and self-satisfied a class of peasantry as ever clustered around a Maypole.

Bill and me had a joint capital of about six hundred dollars, and we needed just two thousand dollars more to pull off a fraudulent town-lot scheme in western Illinois with. We talked it over on the front steps of the hotel. Philoprogenitiveness, says we, is strong in semi-rural communities; therefore, and for other reasons, a kidnapping project ought to do better there than in the radius of newspapers that send reporters out in plain clothes to stir up talk about such things. We knew that Summit couldn't get after us with anything stronger than constables and, maybe, some lackadaisical bloodhounds and a diatribe or two in the *Weekly Farmers' Budget*. So, it looked good.

We selected for our victim the only child of a prominent citizen named Ebenezer Dorset. The father was respectable and tight, a mortgage fancier and a stern, upright collection-plate passer and forecloser. The kid was a boy of ten, with bas-relief freckles, and hair the colour of the cover of the magazine you buy at the news-stand when you want to catch a train. Bill and me figured that Ebenezer would melt down for a ransom of two thousand dollars to a cent. But wait till I tell you.

About two miles from Summit was a little mountain, covered with a dense cedar brake. On the rear elevation of this mountain was a cave. There we stored provisions.

One evening after sundown, we drove in a buggy past old Dorset's house. The kid was in the street, throwing rocks at a kitten on the opposite fence.

'Hey, little boy!' says Bill, 'Would you like to have a bag of candy and a nice ride?'

The boy catches Bill neatly in the eye with a piece of brick.

'That will cost the old man an extra five hundred dollars,' says Bill, climbing over the wheel.

That boy put up a fight like a welterweight cinnamon bear; but, at last, we got him down in the bottom of the buggy and drove away. We took him up to the cave, and I hitched the horse in the cedar brake. After dark I drove the buggy to the little village, three miles away, where we had hired it, and walked back to the mountain.

Bill was pasting court plaster over the scratches and bruises on his features. There was a fire burning behind the big rock at the entrance of the cave, and the boy was watching a pot of boiling coffee, with two buzzard tail feathers stuck in his red hair. He points a stick at me when I come up, and says:

'Ha! cursed paleface, do you dare to enter the camp of Red Chief, the terror of the plains?'

'He's all right now,' says Bill, rolling up his trousers and examining some bruises on his shins. 'We're playing Indian. We're making Buffalo Bill's show look like magic-lantern views of Palestine in the town hall. I'm Old Hank, the Trapper, Red Chief's captive, and I'm to be scalped at daybreak. By Geronimo! that kid can kick hard.'

Yes, sir, that boy seemed to be having the time of his life. The fun of camping out in a cave had made him forget that he was a captive himself. He immediately christened me Snake-eye, the Spy, and announced that, when his braves returned from the warpath, I was to be broiled at the stake at the rising of the sun.

Then we had supper; and he filled his mouth full of bacon and bread and gravy, and began to talk. He made a during-dinner speech something like this:

'I like this fine. I never camped out before; but I had a pet possum once, and I was nine last birthday. I hate to go to school. Rats ate up sixteen of Jimmy Talbot's aunt's speckled hen's eggs. Are there any real Indians in these woods? I want some more gravy. Does the trees moving make the wind blow? We had five puppies. What makes your nose so red, Hank? My father has lots of money. Are the stars hot? I whipped Ed Walker twice, Saturday. I don't like girls. You dassent catch toads unless with a string. Do oxen make any noise? Why are oranges round? Have you got beds to sleep on in this cave? Amos Murray has got six toes. A parrot can talk, but a monkey or a fish can't. How many does it take to make twelve?'

Every few minutes he would remember that he was a pesky redskin, and pick up his stick rifle and tiptoe to the mouth of the cave to rubber for the scouts of the hated paleface. Now and then he would let out a war whoop that made Old Hank the Trapper shiver. That boy had Bill terrorised from the start.

'Red Chief,' says I to the kid, 'would you like to go home?'

'Aw, what for?' says he. 'I don't have any fun at home. I hate to go to school. I like to camp out. You won't take me back home again, Snake-eye, will you?'

'Not right away,' says I. 'We'll stay here in the cave a while.'

'All right!' says he. 'That'll be fine. I never had such fun in all my life.'

We went to bed about 11 o'clock. We spread down some wide blankets and quilts and put Red Chief between us. We weren't afraid he'd run away. He kept us awake for three hours, jumping up and reaching for his rifle and screeching: 'Hist! pard,' in mine and Bill's ears, as the fancied crackle of a twig or the rustle of a leaf revealed to his young imagination the stealthy approach of the outlaw band. At last, I fell into a troubled sleep, and dreamed that I had been kidnapped and chained to a tree by a ferocious pirate with red hair.

Just at daybreak, I was awakened by a series of awful screams from Bill. They weren't yells, or howls, or shouts, or whoops, or yawps, such as you'd expect from a manly set of vocal organs — they were simply indecent, terrifying, humiliating screams, such as women emit when they see ghosts or caterpillars. It's an awful thing to hear a strong, desperate, fat man scream incontinently in a cave at daybreak.

I jumped up to see what the matter was. Red Chief was sitting on Bill's chest with one hand twined in Bill's hair. In the other he had the sharp case knife we used for slicing bacon; and he was industriously and realistically trying to take Bill's scalp, according to the sentence that had been pronounced upon him the evening before.

I got the knife away from the kid and made him lie down again. But, from that moment, Bill's spirit was broken. He laid down on his side of the bed, but he never closed an eye again in sleep as long as that boy was with us. I dozed off for a while, but along toward sun-up I remembered that Red Chief had said I was to be burned at the stake at the rising of the sun. I wasn't nervous or afraid; but I sat up and lit my pipe and leaned against a rock.

'What you getting up so soon for, Sam?' asked Bill.

'Me?' says I. 'Oh, I got a kind of pain in my shoulder. I thought sitting up would rest it.'

'You're a liar!' says Bill. 'You're afraid. You was to be burned at sunrise, and you was afraid he'd do it. And he would, too, if he could find a match. Ain't it awful, Sam? Do you think anybody will pay out money to get a little imp like that back home?'

'Sure,' said I. 'A rowdy kid like that is just the kind that parents dote on. Now, you and the Chief get up and cook breakfast, while I go up on the top of this mountain and reconnoitre.'

I went up on the peak of the little mountain and ran my eye over the contiguous vicinity. Over toward Summit I expected to see the sturdy yeomanry of the village armed with scythes and pitchforks beating the countryside for the dastardly kidnappers. But what I saw was a peaceful landscape dotted with one man ploughing with a dun mule. Nobody was dragging the creek; no couriers dashed hither and yon, bringing tidings of no news to the distracted parents. There was a sylvan attitude of somnolent

sleepiness pervading that section of the external outward surface
of Alabama that lay exposed to my view. 'Perhaps,' says I to
myself, 'it has not yet been discovered that the wolves have
borne away the tender lambkin from the fold. Heaven help the
wolves!' says I, and I went down the mountain to breakfast.

When I got to the cave, I found Bill backed up against the side
of it, breathing hard, and the boy threatening to smash him with
a rock half as big as a coconut.

'He put a red-hot boiled potato down my back,' explained
Bill, 'and then mashed it with his foot; and I boxed his ears.
Have you got a gun about you, Sam?'

I took the rock away from the boy and kind of patched up the
argument. 'I'll fix you,' says the kid to Bill. 'No man ever yet
struck the Red Chief but what he got paid for it. You better
beware!'

After breakfast the kid takes a piece of leather with strings
wrapped around it out of his pocket and goes outside the cave
unwinding it.

'What's he up to now?' says Bill anxiously. 'You don't think
he'll run away, do you, Sam?'

'No fear of it,' says I. 'He don't seem to be much of a
homebody. But we've got to fix up some plan about the ransom.
There don't seem to be much excitement around Summit on
account of his disappearance, but maybe they haven't realised
yet that he's gone. His folks may think he's spending the night
with Aunt Jane or one of the neighbours. Anyhow, he'll be
missed today. Tonight we must get a message to his father
demanding the two thousand dollars for his return.'

Just then we heard a kind of war whoop, such as David might
have emitted when he knocked out the champion Goliath. It
was a sling that Red Chief had pulled out of his pocket, and he
was whirling it around his head.

I dodged, and heard a heavy thud and a kind of a sigh from
Bill, like a horse gives out when you take his saddle off. A rock
the size of an egg had caught Bill just behind his left ear. He
loosened himself all over and fell in the fire across the frying pan
of hot water for washing the dishes. I dragged him out and
poured cold water on his head for half an hour.

By and by, Bill sits up and feels behind his ear and says: 'Sam, do you know who my favourite Biblical character is?'

'Take it easy,' says I. 'You'll come to your senses presently.'

'King Herod,' says he. 'You won't go away and leave me here alone, will you, Sam?'

I went out and caught that boy and shook him until his freckles rattled.

'If you don't behave,' says I, 'I'll take you straight home. Now, are you going to be good, or not?'

'I was only funning,' says he sullenly. 'I didn't mean to hurt Old Hank. But what did he hit me for? I'll behave, Snake-eye, if you won't send me home, and if you'll let me play the Black Scout today.'

'I don't know the game,' says I. 'That's for you and Mr Bill to decide. He's your playmate for the day. I'm going away for a while, on business. Now, you come in and make friends with him and say you are sorry for hurting him, or home you go, at once.'

I made him and Bill shake hands, and then I took Bill aside and told him I was going to Poplar Cove, a little village three miles from the cave, and find out what I could about how the kidnapping had been regarded in Summit. Also, I thought it best to send a peremptory letter to old man Dorset that day, demanding the ransom and dictating how it should be paid.

'You know, Sam,' says Bill, 'I've stood by you without batting an eye in earthquakes, fire, and flood — in poker games, dynamite outrages, police raids, train robberies, and cyclones. I never lost my nerve yet till we kidnapped that two-legged skyrocket of a kid. He's got me going. You won't leave me long with him, will you, Sam?'

'I'll be back some time this afternoon,' says I. 'You must keep the boy amused and quiet till I return. And now we'll write the letter to old Dorset.'

Bill and I got paper and pencil and worked on the letter while Red Chief, with a blanket wrapped around him, strutted up and down, guarding the mouth of the cave. Bill begged me tearfully to make the ransom fifteen hundred dollars instead of two thousand. 'I ain't attempting,' says he, 'to decry the celebrated moral aspect of parental affection, but we're dealing with humans, and it ain't human for anybody to give up two thousand

dollars for that forty-pound chunk of freckled wildcat. I'm
willing to take a chance at fifteen hundred dollars. You can
charge the difference up to me.'

So, to relieve Bill, I acceded, and we collaborated a letter that
ran this way:

> *Ebenezer Dorset, Esq:*
>
> We have your boy concealed in a place far from
> Summit. It is useless for you or the most skilful
> detectives to attempt to find him. Absolutely, the
> only terms on which you can have him restored to
> you are these: We demand fifteen hundred dollars
> in large bills for his return; the money to be left at
> midnight tonight at the same spot and in the same
> box as your reply — as hereinafter described. If
> you agree to these terms, send your answer in
> writing by a solitary messenger tonight at half-past
> eight o'clock. After crossing Owl Creek, on the
> road to Poplar Cove, there are three large trees
> about a hundred yards apart, close to the fence of
> the wheat field on the right-hand side. At the
> bottom of the fence post, opposite the third tree,
> will be found a small pasteboard box.
>
> The messenger will place the answer in this box
> and return immediately to Summit.
>
> If you attempt any treachery or fail to comply
> with our demand as stated, you will never see your
> boy again.
>
> If you pay the money as demanded, he will be
> returned to you safe and well within three hours.
> These terms are final, and if you do not accede to
> them no further communication will be attempted.
>
> *Two Desperate Men*

I addressed this letter to Dorset, and put it in my pocket. As I
was about to start, the kid comes up to me and says:

'Aw, Snake-eye, you said I could play the Black Scout while
you was gone.'

'Play it, of course,' says I. 'Mr Bill will play with you. What kind of a game is it?'

'I'm the Black Scout,' says Red Chief, 'and I have to ride to the stockade to warn the settlers that the Indians are coming. I'm tired of playing Indian myself. I want to be the Black Scout.'

'All right,' says I. 'It sounds harmless to me. I guess Mr Bill will help you foil the pesky savages.'

'What am I to do?' asks Bill, looking at the kid suspiciously.

'You are the hoss,' says Black Scout. 'Get down on your hands and knees. How can I ride to the stockade without a hoss?'

'You'd better keep him interested,' said I, 'till we get the scheme going. Loosen up.'

Bill gets down on his all fours, and a look comes in his eye like a rabbit's when you catch it in a trap.

'How far is it to the stockade, kid?' he asks, in a husky manner of voice.'

'Ninety miles,' says the Black Scout. 'And you have to hump yourself to get there on time. Whoa, now!' The Black Scout jumps on Bill's back and digs his heels in his side.

'For heaven's sake,' says Bill, 'hurry back, Sam, as soon as you can. I wish we hadn't made the ransom more than a thousand. Say, you quit kicking me or I'll get up and warm you good.'

I walked over to Poplar Cove and sat around the post office and store talking with the chaw-bacons that came in to trade. One whiskerando says that he hears Summit is all upset on account of Elder Ebenezer Dorset's boy having been lost or stolen. That was all I wanted to know. I bought some smoking tobacco, referred casually to the price of black-eyed peas, posted my letter surreptitiously, and came away. The postmaster said the mail carrier would come by in an hour to take the mail on to Summit.

When I got back to the cave, Bill and the boy were not to be found. I explored the vicinity of the cave and risked a yodel or two, but there was no response.

So I lighted my pipe and sat down on a mossy bank to await developments.

In about half an hour I heard the bushes rustle, and Bill

wabbled out into the little glade in front of the cave. Behind him
was the kid, stepping softly like a scout, with a broad grin on his
face. Bill stopped, took off his hat, and wiped his face with a red
handkerchief. The kid stopped about eight feet behind him.

'Sam,' says Bill, 'I suppose you'll think I'm a renegade, but I
couldn't help it. I'm a grown person with masculine proclivities
and habits of self-defence, but there is a time when all systems
of egotism and predominance fail. The boy is gone. I have sent
him home. All is off. There was martyrs in old times,' goes on
Bill, 'that suffered death rather than give up the particular graft
they enjoyed. None of 'em ever was subjugated to such supernatural tortures as I have been. I tried to be faithful to our
articles of depredation, but there came a limit.'

'What's the trouble, Bill?' I asks him.

'I was rode,' says Bill, 'the ninety miles to the stockade, not
barring an inch. Then, when the settlers was rescued, I was
given oats. Sand ain't a palatable substitute. And then, for an
hour I had to try to explain to him why there was nothin' in
holes, how a road can run both ways, and what makes the grass
green. I tell you, Sam, a human can only stand so much. I takes
him by the neck of his clothes and drags him down the mountain.
On the way he kicks my legs black-and-blue from the knees
down; and I've got to have two or three bites on my thumb and
hand cauterised.'

'But he's gone' — continues Bill — 'gone home. I showed him
the road to Summit and kicked him about eight feet nearer there
at one kick. I'm sorry we lose the ransom, but it was either that
or Bill Driscoll to the madhouse.'

Bill is puffing and blowing, but there is a look of ineffable
peace and growing content on his rose-pink features.

'Bill,' says I, 'there isn't any heart disease in your family, is
there?'

'No,' says Bill, 'nothing chronic except malaria and accidents.
Why?'

'Then you might turn around,' says I, 'and have a look behind
you.'

Bill turns and sees the boy, and loses his complexion and sits
down plump on the ground and begins to pluck aimlessly at
grass and little sticks. For an hour I was afraid for his mind.
And then I told him that my scheme was to put the whole job

through immediately and that we would get the ransom and be off with it by midnight if old Dorset fell in with our proposition. So Bill braced up enough to give the kid a weak sort of a smile and a promise to play the Russian in a Japanese war with him as soon as he felt a little better.

I had a scheme for collecting that ransom without danger of being caught by counterplots that ought to commend itself to professional kidnappers. The tree under which the answer was to be left — and the money later on — was close to the road fence with big, bare fields on all sides. If a gang of constables should be watching for anyone to come for the note, they could see him a long way off crossing the fields or in the road. But no, siree! At half-past eight I was up in that tree as well hidden as a tree toad, waiting for the messenger to arrive.

Exactly on time, a half-grown boy rides up the road on a bicycle, locates the pasteboard box at the foot of the fence post, slips a folded piece of paper into it, and pedals away again back toward Summit.

I waited an hour and then concluded the thing was square. I slid down the tree, got the note, slipped along the fence till I struck the woods, and was back at the cave in another half an hour. I opened the note, got near the lantern, and read it to Bill. It was written with a pen in a crabbed hand, and the sum and substance of it was this:

Two Desperate Men

Gentlemen: I received your letter today by post, in regard to the ransom you ask for the return of my son. I think you are a little high in your demands, and I hereby make you a counterproposition, which I am inclined to believe you will accept. You bring Johnny home and pay me two hundred and fifty dollars in cash, and I agree to take him off your hands. You had better come at night, for the neighbours believe he is lost, and I couldn't be responsible for what they would do to anybody they saw bringing him back.

Very respectfully,

Ebenezer Dorset

'Great pirates of Penzance!' says I, 'of all the impudent—'

But I glanced at Bill and hesitated. He had the most appealing look in his eyes I ever saw on the face of a dumb or a talking brute.

'Sam,' says he, 'what's two hundred and fifty dollars, after all? We've got the money. One more night of this kid will send me to a bed in Bedlam. Besides being a thorough gentleman, I think Mr Dorset is a spendthrift for making us such a liberal offer. You ain't going to let the chance go, are you?'

'Tell you the truth, Bill,' says I, 'this little he ewe lamb has somewhat got on my nerves too. We'll take him home, pay the ransom, and make our getaway.'

We took him home that night. We got him to go by telling him that his father had bought a silver-mounted rifle and a pair of moccasins for him, and we were going to hunt bears the next day.

It was just twelve o'clock when we knocked at Ebenezer's front door. Just at the moment when I should have been abstracting the fifteen hundred dollars from the box under the tree, according to the original proposition, Bill was counting out two hundred and fifty dollars into Dorset's hand.

When the kid found out we were going to leave him at home, he started up a howl like a calliope and fastened himself as tight as a leech to Bill's leg. His father peeled him away gradually, like a porous plaster.

'How long can you hold him?' asks Bill.

'I'm not as strong as I used to be,' says old Dorset, 'but I think I can promise you ten minutes.'

'Enough,' says Bill. 'In ten minutes I shall cross the Central, Southern, and Middle Western States and be legging it trippingly for the Canadian border.'

And, as dark as it was, and as fat as Bill was, and as good a runner as I am, he was a good mile and a half out of Summit before I could catch up with him.

FARRUKH DHONDY

Salt on a Snake's Tail

There was the short route home from school and the long route. Jolil took the long route because by the time he got out of school the other boys who lived in his building had gone home. Mr Morrisson had kept him behind in his office and shown him some books.

'We must do something about your English,' Mr Morrisson had said. 'Come up to my room at ten to four and we'll go over some things together.'

Jolil didn't want to refuse. He didn't want to tell Mr Morrisson why he was impatient to get home. He usually left the school gate with five or six of the other Asian boys. It wasn't planned, but it was necessary. If they walked home together, they could pass the gangs of older white boys who gathered outside the school gates without fear. They'd take the short route home, and if they passed the cluster of hostile faces outside the white estate at the end of their street, they could quicken their steps and feel the safe warmth of being part of a crowd. If you walked past there alone, you walked along the Whitechapel Road and came round to the flats the long way.

'I got something out of the public library specially for you, Jolil,' Mr Morrisson said, and he handed Jolil a book on the martial arts. He had told Mr Morrisson some days before that that was what he was interested in.

'Don't just stare at the pictures, try and read some of it,' Mr Morrisson said.

His father saw him clutching the thick book when he got home. 'Go wash your face and say your prayers,' Mr Miah said.

'We're not going to the mosque till later,' Jolil protested. He headed for the inside room where he and his sisters slept. His father was already wearing his white muslin prayer cap. A bad sign, Jolil thought. It meant that his dad was in a lecturing mood. He would carry on at him.

'Get down to *namaaz*,' he said sternly. 'The devout must pray as many times on Friday as they can. There is no help for us but Allah. Who did you come home with?'

Jolil didn't reply. He sat on his bed and opened the book that Mr Morrisson had given him. Normally when he got home, his father would be working at the machines in the front room, sewing acres of cloth together, fulfilling the 'contract'. But Friday was the sabbath. The machines would stop. The women would be in the kitchen, his mother and sister-in-law. His father would prowl about the front room and give directives which most of them ignored.

Jolil had let Mr Morrisson into the secret. He had told him why he liked Kung Fu and Bruce Lee.

'Read anything, read comics if you must,' Mr Morrisson said. He didn't really catch on, Jolil thought, it was another reading exercise to him. His friend Errol knew about Kung Fu; he'd take him the book when he went over to his place on Saturday.

Jolil turned the pages. Bruce Lee's muscles almost bulged out of the photographs. His hands, fingers outstretched, seemed to be clawing magical strength out of the very air. The red scars on his body were supposed to be blood wounds, but they looked deliberately cut in neat patterns. And his face, Jolil thought, his face had the authoritative power of a humble man. Jolil tried to read the writing on the opposite page. He could read each word, but the sentences didn't seem to add up. The pictures couldn't actually tell you how to put the thing into practice, but they told a story all right. Bruce Lee was a simple man, probably a poor

man when he started out. He even wore the clothes of an
urchin, two sizes too small for a grown man. In one picture, he
was in the air, a fierce animal, falling with puma-like fists on
four shocked opponents.

Jolil rose from the bed and went to the mantelshelf and
looked in the mirror. His mother came into the room and took
the brass box of betel nut and cloth in which the betel leaves
were wrapped.

'Go and wash your face, your father will be furious,' she said.
Jolil narrowed his eyes and undid three buttons on his shirt,
staring into the mirror. He touched his cheek-bones. Yes, they
were somewhat like Bruce Lee's.

'You bring this book of idols into the house?' his father
suddenly asked. Jolil lowered his arms and turned round. His
father had picked the book up off the bed and was leafing
through it with an expression of severe disapproval. Mr Miah
did a dry, coughing gargle in his throat, as though gathering his
spit to show his contempt.

'It's from school,' Jolil said.

'Who leads young men astray with all these pictures of half-
naked actors?' Jolil's father asked. 'Who is it that teaches young
men this sort of disrespect?'

'Give it to me. I'll put it away,' Jolil said, trying to take the
book from his father's hands.

'You should be reading the Koran. I shall still be grateful to
Allah, even though he's given me an infidel son. You'd better
read the books that matter, son, before you take up all these
Chinaman's tricks. You don't reply when your father asks you
questions anymore, eh?'

'What questions?' Jolil asked, trying to distract his father's
attention while he grabbed the book and looked around for a
hiding place for it.

'Who did you come home from school with?'

'Errol.'

'Errol, eh? Well, it's time you stopped running around with
the darkies. You should be down in the basement learning to
read Arabic with Kazi-sahab.'

'All the babies go to Kazi's class,' Jolil replied.

'You are never too old to humble yourself and learn the
words of Allah.'

'Anyway, I know Arabic. I know Urdu . . .aleph, be, pe, the, zaal, zin and everything.'

'The only Urdu you know is from those rubbish films. You have no respect, bringing rubbish books into the house, and dirty pictures of actors and Chinamen.'

'He's not an actor,' Jolil said. 'He's a tiger.'

'A common wrestler. Tigers are stupid creatures anyway. They live outside the grace of God; they fall into pits built with twigs and leaves to trap them.'

Jolil knew when his father was about to begin some story about Bangladesh. He'd heard this one twenty times, about the tiger who thought that every trodden path had been paved by his own paws and was surprised to find a monkey loping along the cleared track to his water-hole. Jolil didn't want to hear the end of it. He turned and went into the kitchen and asked his sister-in-law when his brother would be home.

'He's gone to the meeting.'

'They always have these useless meetings. They are becoming Godless in this wretched country; they think they can fight white men. You know how many white men there are?' his father asked, walking into the kitchen. The women made no reply.

'I wanted to go to the meeting,' Jolil said.

'They will talk. Bengalis love to talk big talk,' his father said.

There had been an incident in the previous week. A Bengali had been stabbed in the ear on his way home from work. The white gang that stabbed him had run away. Some people in the flats where Jolil's family lived had called a meeting of all the families. His elder brother, Khalil, had gone and returned with the news that they were planning some defence of their buildings. The night of the stabbing, gangs of Bengali youths had set out from the cafés on Brick Lane, determined to challenge any white gang that offered insult or violence. Then the next day someone had thrown a brick through the window of the ground-floor flat and another meeting had been called, this time of the whole building.

'If they want a war, there's going to be a war,' Khalil said when he returned.

'What can you do if God's will is not with you?'

'Leave God aside,' Khalil replied. 'We're going to store bricks and stones on the terrace, and if a gang turns up to attack, we can all go up there and deal with them.'

'If a snake stings you once, you don't turn round and chase it so it can sting you again. Leave it alone,' Mr Miah said to his eldest son.

'What do you do if it turns round to sting you again?'

'You put salt on its tail,' Mr Miah said.

He always said that sort of thing as though it were God's truth. Sometimes Jolil wanted to argue with him. He couldn't make sense of his dad's proverbs. His dad would say, each grain of rice bears the name of the person who's destined to eat it. Or he'd say, you put salt on a snake's tail and it'll never bother you again. Another day he'd shout at Jolil for spilling grains of salt on the kitchen floor while sprinkling his chips and tell him that when he appeared before God, he would be made to pick up every grain of salt he'd wasted in his lifetime with his eyelids before he'd be allowed past the gates of heaven. It was all nonsense.

But Mr Miah used a no-nonsense tone to say it in. They were the truths of life, just like going to the mosque on Fridays, and working at the machine when your father told you to.

Jolil would only assist with the sewing work when a contract had to be urgently finished. He'd skip school and help his father and sister-in-law who sat all day at the two machines in their front room. When a contract was 'urgent', the machines would spread their clatter into the night. Jolil didn't like machining, but he wouldn't tell his dad. Mr Miah said there were two types of money, sweat money and water money, and with water money you couldn't keep a family alive, you could only gamble it away or buy water with it. You had to sweat if you wanted to eat. Jolil would load the thread on to the machines, he'd wind up reels of nylon and separate sewn pieces from the piles of cut material every hour, he'd fetch the tea and he'd run down to the shop for condensed milk and cigarettes when he was asked to.

'You'll have to miss school on Monday and work at these linings,' his father said.

'Why can't we finish it over the week-end?'

'We don't work on the sabbath,' Mr Miah said, 'and on

Sunday we're going to Dog Market to get some chairs. We have to get your mother some chairs.'

'I have to go to school on Monday.'

'What for? Since when have you become so fond of learning?'

'They're going to show a Kung Fu film to all the third years.'

'They waste your time in school,' his father said. 'What use is that to you in becoming a tailor?'

'It's not an ordinary film,' Jolil said. 'It's about the secrets of Kung Fu. Mr Morrisson is bringing a film which will explain everything.'

'Everything can never be explained,' his father said. 'If you carry on in this useless way, I'll send you back to Bangladesh and you can learn to be a begging wrestler, go from village to village and challenge all the idiots to fight.'

'I'll work tomorrow. I can do a hundred linings in a day,' Jolil said.

He'd do it, he thought. When they'd been at the old house, there was still some joy left in this business, making the needle hum between your fingers. Tailoring made nimble but tired fingers. It turned your fingers into tools. Kung Fu converted them into weapons.

These were thoughts his father wouldn't understand. In a movie called *The Black Dragon Revenges the Death of Bruce Lee*, the hero had plucked out the eyes of several villains and destroyed with similar cruelty the faces of others. There was a knack to it. You twisted your palm in the faces of the enemy. Your hurricane hands had to be trained to lay low an army of fiends. Once he was good enough, Jolil told himself, he'd allow people to photograph him. That's the kind of hero he wanted to be. Once he was good enough he'd get his photograph in the *Martial Arts* magazine, and in *Filmfare*, which his sister-in-law read. He'd be the first Bangladeshi martial arts hero, and his films would sell better than those of Rajesh Khanna, whom his sister-in-law adored, and then he could buy a big white American car. But if he ever became famous, he wouldn't go and live in Malabar Hill in Bombay like the other film stars did. He'd use his powers to do other things, to right a lot of wrongs, to be a saint of the fighting world.

His father had once told Jolil a story about a wise man being reborn in a remote village in Sylhet. He said the souls of old bandits implanted themselves in the bodies of newborn babies and returned as flesh in the families of saintly people. Wisdom passes from man to man, his father said. Strength is God-given and can't be extinguished; it's like a flame which leaves not only embers but heat behind it. And Jolil wondered whether the soul of Bruce Lee would pass into the body of an up-and-coming young hero. It was one of his father's stories that he wanted to believe.

In the past few months, Mr Miah had come up with a lot of these stories. Jolil had noticed that the more trouble there was, the more philosophical his father became. He would put on his prayer-cap and he would mutter at the rest of the family. Khalil had stopped paying any attention to him.

Khalil said there'd be more trouble. When the summer came the whites would go on the rampage, they'd maybe come with guns. Khalil's mates all said that they wanted to be ready, but Jolil knew that they didn't know how to be ready for them. The first task was to protect their building. There were fifty Bengali families there. They were all squatters. They had moved into the building amid tremendous excitement. Some young Bengalis had moved the first family in, and the news had spread through Brick Lane and its environs. Like the rest, Jolil's family had quit their little back room in their relatives' house and moved their mattresses and utensils to the new place. It wasn't new at all, of course. It was an old building that nobody else wanted. On the first day there had been a lot of coming and going. The police came and white men from the government came in vans and spoke to the two or three young men who were conducting the whole operation. They had settled in and a month later the trouble began. Some of the Bengalis were very fierce. They'd make tough speeches about fighting and about protecting their families and their own people. Jolil's father didn't make any speeches, at least not in public. He argued with Khalil at home.

Khalil would say, 'This is a *jehad*, a holy war. If we want to stay in this country, we have to fight.'

And yet Khalil brushed his hair to look like a film star and put on his best clothes and went out with his friends, strolling up and down Whitechapel Road and Brick Lane and making trips to the West End. Even Khalil didn't understand what it was they had to do. Strolling around Brick Lane wouldn't make you strong, wouldn't build you up and strike terror in the guts of the 'rubbish' whites. Jolil was determined to practise the arts of discipline and meditation, because Mr Morrisson had told him that being an expert at anything was difficult. At the root of all strength was discipline and meditation. But how was it to be done? He'd hit the palm of his hand against the wall a hundred times and count to a hundred because the counting kept his mind off the pain.

When he was indoors, or outside in the courtyard with the younger children from their building, he'd practise his kicks. He'd try and raise his knee higher each time, flicking his foot out from under, imitating lightning. He still struggled to retain his balance. One day he'd be perfect. He'd go to Kung Fu classes and win himself a black belt.

Jolil knew that Errol was also training. And Errol had learnt modesty. He'd never show off in the playground at school. He wouldn't raise a fist or a leg. But Jolil knew that Errol had hardened his palms with careful persistence and he could break planks of wood at a stroke if he wanted. He showed Jolil how to twist his fist when he pushed it out to arm's length. That was one of the secrets. It was a controlled, graceful movement and you had to learn to get it just right. And fast. Speed was another secret. Silence was yet another. Strength was more terrifying if it wasn't expected. You had to look like a priest and fight like a tiger. Then there was confidence. One of the reasons Jolil didn't practise his strokes in front of Errol or any of the other boys in school, was that they might laugh at him. When they laughed, your spirit got soaked up, and then no matter how fast and rough your fists were, you'd be defeated by their stares and their grins. Your confidence had to defeat those stares and grins.

'Put your cap on, we're going to prayers,' Mr Miah said. Jolil got his jacket on and put his prayer-cap in his pocket. He wasn't going into the street with it on. His father strode slightly ahead of him. It was still light when they came out of the flats and passed under the old archway. His father turned left. They were going to take the route past the white estate. The younger children were still playing in the courtyard. They wandered around the piles of debris and stalked through the deserted basements, climbing in and out through window sills with their frames ripped out. Their voices, a mixture of Bengali and sharp English exclamations, echoed round the yard. The sound of sewing machines and the odour of frying spices floated out of open doorways.

'You hear them?' Jolil's father said. 'They won't stop their machines for judgement day. They shouldn't call themselves Muslims. See what the promise of a few pence does to our people?'

He gathered his spit and fired it out of his mouth on to the pavement. They walked across the narrow cobbled street, past the boarded-up warehouses towards the mosque. Jolil knew that the kids from the white estate at the end of that street called this territory 'Paki-land'. They'd have to pass through those shabby concrete flats and then they'd be safe again. The new concrete would give way again to the half-gutted complex of old factories and houses, the smell of 'pig-lard' as his father called it in Bengali, would give way again to the richer scents of garlic and coriander from the warren of Asian dwellings which surrounded the territory of the mosque.

Jolil saw them, and saw that his father had spotted them too: a group of about a dozen white boys and girls, leaning against and sitting on the concrete parapets that surrounded their estate. They should have gone the other way round, Jolil thought. He took a couple of hurried steps to walk abreast of his father. His father's steps became shorter and faster. He was staring straight into space, as though he was unaware of the eyes of the crowd that greeted their approach. A small lump came into Jolil's throat. It wasn't too late to turn round and go the other way, even if it meant an extra half-mile to walk. But that was what they mustn't do. His father walked on as though the thought hadn't occurred to him.

As they approached, the gang stopped their chatter. They stood sultry and silent. Jolil looked at their feet as he passed, he didn't want to look up in their faces in case they took that as a provocation. They looked massive, these white youths, in their close-fitting clothes and their close-cropped hair.

'Allah will guide us,' Jolil's father muttered, as though to himself.

They walked past the gang and a voice called out from behind them, 'Oi, Pak-a-mac.'

'Keep walking,' Jolil's father said to him, pretending to be in charge of their pace which was light with the lift of fear. Jolil could see that his father was afraid. Maybe even this gang of louts could smell the stink of funk that came off him.

'Can't wait now, eh?' one of the boys said. 'Got to rush off and put in some overtime.' He was trying to imitate an Asian accent.

'Leave off, Baz,' one of the girls on the parapet said. 'One of these days these blokes are going to lay a hiding on you.'

'Don't make me laugh,' the boy said. 'The only hiding these geezers know is under their beds when there's trouble. Even that won't help them soon, though.'

Mr Miah's step had broken into a kind of run.

'You'll have to run all the way back to the jungle,' a voice from the mob shouted behind them.

'You see why the Koran forbids us to drink?' asked Jolil's father. Jolil didn't reply.

At the mosque Jolil tried to concentrate on his prayers. His heart was still beating fast. What could they have done, he was thinking. He looked round at the other men who were on their knees, bending their bodies to the intonation of the prayers. Jolil felt a sense of calm. All these people, he thought, all these people. They can't drive us anywhere. Khalil had said that the whites wanted to drive them back by scaring them, making them so afraid to walk the streets that they'd have to pack up and go back to Bangladesh.

He looked up at his father. His panic seemed to have passed away and he looked serenely absorbed in his prayers, opening and closing his eyes. A little threat, a little discomfort, that was what life offered you, he seemed to be thinking. Jolil knew his father. To him it wasn't important. Maybe it wasn't important to all this crowd on their knees. Like the snow and the early dark in winter, this threat and hatred that had been loosed all round their surrounded lives, was just part of the fact of England. Like the kites in the skies over the villages in Bangladesh, or the locusts that swept the crops, coming like the monsoon in

fatal clouds, these 'rubbish whites' as they called them, were
creatures with whom one had to share the landscape. For Jolil
they were different. For six years he'd been to school with white
kids. He knew every twist of the language they spoke. He
understood the jokes they made. He knew their reasons and
their unreason. To his father they were people to be ignored,
their remarks were like the noise of crows in the trees towards
sunset; they signified nothing.

After coming out of the mosque, Jolil noticed that his father
lingered around until they were joined in the street by other men
from their building.

'Never be scared of jackals,' he said to Jolil. 'If those white
men had tried to attack us or anything I would have taught
them a good lesson.'

'We should go round the other way,' Jolil said.

'Oh no,' his father replied. 'Streets were made to walk on.'
And he spat with conviction.

'You should have spat at them when they abused us,' Jolil
said.

'My mouth was dry, boy.'

The next afternoon Jolil was at Errol's place. Errol's room was
plastered with Kung Fu posters. Jolil told Errol about the book
that Mr Morrisson had given him.

'Some high books on Kung Fu, boy, only black belts could
understand them. It ain't like foo'ball where anyone can see the
tricks. Kung Fu is a heavy science, boy; if you don't know the
meditation, then you can't do nothing,' Errol said.

They discussed the film they were going to see. Morrisson had
told them that it was called *The Secrets of Kung Fu*. Errol said
maybe the film could teach him a couple of things, there were
still one or two things he needed to know.

When Jolil got home his father and sister-in-law were at the
machines. His father would normally give up his seat to Jolil
and go off to the mosque on his own, leaving Jolil to work for a
couple of hours. This day he didn't budge. He turned to his
daughter-in-law and said she could have a rest now that Jolil
had returned. They worked in silence. His father hadn't told the
others at home about the incident the previous evening.

On Sunday Jolil set out with his father to Dog Market. It was crowded. People walked between rows of junk shops on either side. The stalls sold everything from vegetables to antique gramophones. His father poked his head into several second-hand shops and looked around for a set of chairs.

'Wanting chair, good chair,' he said to the man with the huge belly who sat outside one of the shops.

'What sort of chairs?'

'For sitting down.'

'Look in there, mate, I've got plenty of chairs.'

'How much price?'

His father walked to the back of the shop which was piled with mattresses and old tables and canvas sheets and broken furniture. He lifted a well-polished chair off the top of the pile.

'Those are no good to you, mate,' the man said. 'They're antiques.'

'How much?' his father insisted.

'What's the point of telling you if you ain't gonna want them?'

'I want them,' Mr Miah said. Jolil could see that his father understood that this shopkeeper was trying to insult him.

'All right, let's say twelve pound each, all right? Satisfied?'

Mr Miah put the chair back on top of the pile.

'Come and have a dekko at these, mate, more your sort of thing. Good strong chairs, these, last till your boy has grandchildren running all over Spitalfields. They're two quid each,' the man added, handing the steel-framed, plastic-covered chairs to Mr Miah. He dusted the chairs off.

Mr Miah handed over the money.

'I know your people, mate. I know what they like,' the man said.

Jolil took one chair and his father took the other. They passed through the crowd.

'You've got to know how to get things at their proper price — these traders are very sharp,' his father said to Jolil as they emerged from the bustle of the market. Jolil knew they'd been insulted, the man had jeered at them. He walked with his eyes on the pavement. There was no way a man could swallow an insult and still look the world in the eye. One day, he thought, one day he'd be ready. He wouldn't accept walking in fear.

As they turned down Chicksand Street, on the last lap home, pausing every few yards and transferring the awkward weight of the chairs from arm to arm, Jolil saw two of the youths who had been in the gang on Friday night. They were standing on the pavement, leaning against the wall as they had done that night.

'These rubbish people are still there,' his father said. 'When they are in ones and twos they are not so bold, eh? I'll smash this chair over their heads if they say anything to me.' He was strolling with confidence now.

'Men should be as afraid of killing as they are of dying,' he said, and gathering his spit, he spat on the pavement.

'What are you spittin' outside our flats for?' one of the white boys said as they approached them.

'Leave it, leave it, leave it,' Mr Miah said in English.

'I'll give you leave it,' one of the boys said, stepping forward as they passed him.

'Just keep walking, just hold the chair out if he comes,' Mr Miah said in Bengali to Jolil.

The youth was upon them. He grabbed Mr Miah's jacket collar from the back. He tried to wrench loose, dropping his chair. The boy wore a red sweater, and its tightness made his muscles look menacingly large. There was a flash of spite in his face.

'Oi, you want to go and clean up that gob you made there.'

'No, thank you,' said Jolil's father, hastily. 'Just move on, hurry on,' he added, in Bengali, to Jolil.

'Ah, no-speak-d-English, eh? You know damn well what I said, now come back here and clean it up.'

The other youth came strolling up and positioned himself in front of Jolil's father.

'You ain't bolting anywhere, curly-caps,' he said. 'You're going to do as my mate says and clean up your gob.'

He picked up the chair that Mr Miah had dropped and banged it emphatically on the pavement. Then he sat on it.

'Why you trouble an old man?' Jolil's father said. He was beginning to plead. Suddenly Jolil felt he couldn't take it any more. 'Get off, it's our chair,' he said, rushing up to the seated youth and trying to pull the chair from under him.

'You want to digest your teeth, Paki junior?' the youth said.

'It's a very young boy, little boy,' his father said, holding up his hand as if in surrender. He walked back to the place where he'd spat and began shuffling his shoes over the pavement.

'I said with your tongue, not with your Tesco bombers,' the young man said.

Jolil picked up the chair he'd been carrying, lifted it and rushed at the young man. He nimbly stepped aside, jerked the chair out of Jolil's hands and flung it a few yards off. Then he jumped on Jolil and slapped him with his open hands on both cheeks, pushing him off as Jolil rushed at him in between the resounding flat blows.

'Don't you get funny with me,' the youth said between his teeth. Jolil threw himself at him again. The youth got him by the front of his shirt, held him at arms' length and flung him to the ground. Then he pounced on him, kicking him, as Jolil tried to cover his face.

Then he heard his father's voice behind the young man.

'Very sorry, very sorry,' he was saying, and then in Urdu, 'in the name of all-seeing Allah.'

The youth who was kicking Jolil let out a little yelp.

'Aaaah, you bastard,' Jolil heard him say, and he fell to his knees as though he had dropped something on the pavement. Jolil's father screamed at him to run, to leave the chairs. He scrambled to his feet and ran after his father. For a few seconds the other youth ran behind them and then he turned and went back to his companion who was still kneeling on the pavement, screaming as though he had looked in the face of murder. Jolil didn't turn. Neither he nor his father stopped till they reached the broken archway of their own building.

Khalil was at home when they walked in.

'What about the chairs?' his mother asked, and then, seeing the red marks on Jolil's face, 'Oh, my God, what's happened to you?'

'We couldn't find any chairs,' his father said. 'Jolil tripped and fell down as we were coming back.'

'I didn't,' Jolil shouted. 'We ran . . .' he started to say.

'Don't call your father a liar,' Mr Miah said. 'Go inside and wash your face.'

'Why did you run away?' Khalil demanded. 'Who chased you? I'll kill them.'

'I'm not a man of violence,' his father said, 'and the day that sons of mine can tell their father what to do, is the day I want to stop living.'

'If you live like a rat you've already stopped living,' Khalil said.

'Don't answer back, boy. Nobody's been hurt. We're all right. Allah has brought us safely home.'

Khalil wasn't going to speak against Allah. He turned on his heel and walked out of the house.

Jolil's face was burning now, with the slap and with the shame he felt. He didn't venture to tell his mother what had happened. He felt they had lost more than the chairs; they had lost the right to walk on the street. They had lost face. His feet, which should have been shooting kicks at the jaws of danger, had followed each other hastily home.

That night he lay on his back awake, his mind filled with the rage of their helplessness. The house was dark, the rest of the family asleep. Jolil heard a noise in the kitchen. He heard the tap running and the sound of feet trying to tiptoe and then the sound of creaking wood. He got up from his bed and went through the front room quietly and peered into the kitchen. His father was kneeling on the floor in the dark. He turned his head over his shoulder, startled at Jolil's approach.

'Go back to sleep,' he said, sternly.

Jolil stood in the darkened doorway, not obeying his father. The dirty lino on the floor of the kitchen had been turned up, and his father was fiddling with a hammer with one of the floorboards. 'Listen, son,' he said, getting to his feet and turning round, whispering almost. 'Don't ever tell anyone, not even your mother or Khalil, that we bought any chairs or about those men.'

'I won't,' Jolil said. They had run away; he didn't want to tell anyone that his father was a coward. 'Don't worry. I won't.'

The next morning his mother brought some white paste she'd made up and put it on Jolil's cheek. Jolil washed it off, brushed his hair, and, taking the long route, went to school.

In the darkness of the sports' hall, the kids whistled and cheered as Bruce Lee appeared on the screen, leaping over walls, dodging out of the path of bullets, tackling six of his enemies at the same time and laying them flat. Then the film turned from colour to black-and-white. A man in a suit was addressing the audience. '. . . so we take a look at the world in which the stars of this international cult live. We look at the way in which this game is played, we look at the magic and illusion of Kung Fu . . .' There were more shots of men lopping off other men's heads with the swipe of a braced palm. The blood flowed and the third year cheered. Then the white man came on the screen again. He was going to explain, Jolil thought, he was going to give away the secret. As he talked, the picture showed the crew of a film studio setting things up in the background. Then the Chinese man, to whom the white man had been talking, jumped off a wall on which he was perched. The cameramen recorded the jump. The man threw his arms out as he leapt. The white commentator held the film up to the audience.

'So we play it backwards,' he said. The film inside the film was played backwards and it showed the same jump in reverse, looking like the Chinese man had jumped up on to the wall.

Jolil watched it in silence. The film moved to other rooms in the studio. An actor posed next to a dummy of himself.

'Ain't it good,' one of the boys next to him said.

The dummy's head was struck off, the fountains of blood began to pour from it, and its neck was held up to the camera to show how the blood was made to gush out of a pen-sized capsule. 'All this happens at twenty-four frames a second in an ordinary film, the speed of normal life. What happens when you slow the camera down?' There was another shot of the Chinese man aiming kicks to the jaws of other actors. He did it slowly, deliberately, and the director of the film posed the extras in expressions of surprise. There was another shot of the same action at what seemed to be incredible speed.

'Celluloid has created the Kung Fu superman, running, leaping and fighting with fists of speeded-up fury.'

The whole film was like that. When the lights were switched on and Mr Morrisson came to the front of the hall and said that they'd have ten minutes extra on their lunchtime, Jolil turned to

Errol. Most of the others were indifferent to what they had seen.

'In the book that Morrisson gave me, it said that Bruce Lee could really jump on to a ten-foot wall.'

'Bruce Lee dead,' Errol replied.

'It's stupid, I reckon,' said another boy in their row. 'Kung Fu is for mongs.'

'White man spoil everything,' Errol said.

Jolil didn't stay to school in the afternoon. He went back home. He couldn't make up his mind about how he felt about the shattered secret. Maybe the film was lying, all Kung Fu was not like that, it wasn't all tricks.

When he got to their building, Jolil could see three police cars parked outside. There were policemen in the courtyard and several people from the flats were outside talking to them. The women and children leaned out of the windows.

Jolil burst through the door of their flat. His father was sitting at the machine, his spectacles sliding down his nose.

'What's going on here? What're the police doing in our buildings?'

'You want to mind the world's business? You'll have to have a million lives.'

'A white boy was stabbed at the end of the street yesterday evening,' Khalil said. Khalil was looking out of their window. 'The police want to know if any of the children found a knife or anything in the street while playing.'

'Why should we get involved in white man's quarrels?' his father said, threading the machine after licking the thread.

'It wasn't a white man who stabbed him,' Khalil said. 'It was some Bengalis and they left some chairs behind on the pavement.'

'Don't talk loosely, letting your tongue wag in your head. We've got all the chairs we need in this house,' his father said, still at the machine.

Then he turned to Jolil. 'Go and take two pounds from my purse and go down to Brick Lane and buy me a pair of cutters' scissors. Take the long route.'

Personal Essay
by Farrukh Dhondy

In my ideal literary world the writer and the reader are separated only by a mirror. The writer's state of mind, expression, elation, anguish, even actions as he or she writes are reflected exactly in the reader's mind, emotions, nervous system. The reader should, in the moments of reading and contemplation, become the writer. The closest parallel in our culture to this creative-receptive partnership is that of the pop singer or group. The singer sings for the audience and the ideal audience, entranced, believes that the symptoms the singer manifests with passion are symptoms they feel themselves. It is not only Robert Flack who feels that he is 'killing her softly with his song'.

That ideal world doesn't exist. The writer writes and the reader does all sorts of things. The reader may be interested, bored, convinced or sceptical. He or she may be compelled by teachers or syllabuses to graze in unlikely pastures. The critic, which every student reader becomes, compares, responds and criticises. The mirror is shattered. It was an illusion, another setback to the hope that once the cipher of language is decoded we all share the same broad humanity. The writer remains the person who has bothered to say something, the reader retains the privilege of remaining a mystery.

If the ideas worked, writers would never be asked to contribute prefaces. No-one would write biographies of them. The reader would never need to know, in any supplementary form, the experience that made the writer come to that story. So here's another story: when I was a teacher and had just published a collection of short stories entitled *Come To Mecca*, of which 'Salt on a Snake's Tail' is one, I was invited to speak to a group of senior school students by a friend, a fellow teacher. I arrived at his school an hour and a half early, having driven down a motorway faster than I had expected, and was sat in a corner of the staff room awaiting my audience. My friend thought it would be a good and mischievous exercise for me to answer an exam paper which his head of department had set on a few of my stories. I wrote the paper. He put a false pupil's name and number on it and sent it in for correction and marking. Three weeks later he sent me the marked copy. I got a C+ and some praise in red ink for my attempt to understand what the author was getting at. I was also rapped on the knuckles for 'reading too much fanciful political stuff' into my own stories.

I shed no tears for the A+ I should have got. The mistake I made in answering the paper was trying to imagine a reader who would try to imagine the writer's experience. The reading and writing of short stories is not done that way. Though one should be cautious of the sweeping statement, short stories do not recreate an experience. There's not enough time to do that. Novels may attempt it, but short stories are closer to tricks — magicians's turns when they convince, advertiser's chicanery when they fail. They are rarely about what *did* happen; almost always about what *might* have happened if an inventive mind were in charge of that particular universe. Short stories start in observation and are built through invention.

To risk another general statement, novels (though one can think of exceptions and the ones that are set on syllabusses are usually the exceptions) are not directed towards a purpose. Short stories usually are. When I read a short story in English, whether it be British or American, I usually ask myself the question 'so what?' And back comes an answer of a rather complex sort. Stories written outside this modern English or European tradition have even more of a point to make. The best known fables, parables and cautionary tales were invented to press home a point. The reader is meant to take away from them an idea, a dilemma or a question at least. Very many of the stories written in India, Africa or Iran, however modern they are in composition and style, are proud of making a point, of sending the reader away with proof of an idea.

A short story written about non-English settlers in England is expected, almost obliged to make an 'anti-racist' point. Just because it's about blacks or Asians, it is seen as operating in a world of beliefs. The reader will inevitably ask him or herself if this piece of prose does what is expected of it: does it explain blacks to whites; does it give the outsider an insight into the workings of an intimate culture; does it challenge 'stereotypes'?

These are the wrong questions to ask of a short story. They are boring questions to ask the author of a short story. The only two questions to ask are: 'Does this piece of invention convince me, through the accuracy of the writer's ear and eye, that it exists?' and 'Do the characters in it learn any lessons about each other or life?'

ROBERT WESTALL

The Vacancy

It was in a side-street, in the window of a little brown-brick office. Neatly written, on fresh clean card:

> VACANCY AVAILABLE.
> FOR A BRIGHT KEEN LAD.

Martin pulled up, surveyed it suspiciously. Why specify a lad? Illegal, under the Sex-discrimination Act. England was a land of equal opportunity; to be unemployed. Martin laughed, without mirth. The employment-police would be on to that straight away, and he didn't want to get involved with the employment police. But perhaps the employment-police wouldn't bother coming down here. It was such a dingy lost little street. In all his travels he'd never come across a street so lost.

He parked his bike against the dull brown wall. An early 1980s racing-bike, his pride and joy. Salvaged from the conveyor-belt to the metal-eater in the nick of time, rusty and wheelless. He'd haunted the metal-eater for months after that, watching for spare-parts. The security cameras round the metal-eater watched him; or *seemed* to watch him. They moved constantly, but you could never tell if they were on automatic.

Anyway, he'd rebuilt the bike; resprayed it. Spent three months' unemployment benefit on oil and aerosols. Now it shone, and got him round from district to district. The district gate-police didn't like him wheeling it through, but it wasn't illegal. The government hadn't bothered making bikes illegal, just stopped production altogether, including spare-parts. Cycling had imperceptibly died out.

You had to be careful, travelling from district to district. In some, the unemployed threw stones and worse. In others, it was said, they strung up strangers from lamp-posts, as government spies. Though that was probably a rumour spread by the gate-police. He'd never suffered more than the odd, half-hearted stone, even in the beginning. Now, they all knew his bike, gathered round to get the news.

But he'd travelled far that morning, further than ever before, because of the row with his father.

'Your constant moaning makes me sick,' the old man had said, putting on his worker's cap with the numbered brass badge. 'I keep you — you get free sport, free contraceptives, free drugs and a twenty-channel telly. You lie in bed till tea-time. At your age . . .'

'You had a job,' shouted Martin. 'In 1981, at the age of sixteen you were given a job, which you still have.'

'Some job. Two hours a day. Four times in two hours a bloody bell rings and I check a load of dials and write the numbers in a book that nobody needs and nobody reads. Call that a job for a trained electrician?'

'You have a reason to get up in the morning — mates at work.'

'*Mates*? I see the fore-shift when I clock on, and the back-shift when I clock off. My nearest *mate* is ten minutes' walk away. Where *you* going?'

'Out. On my bike.'

'You think you're so bloody clever wi' that bike. *And* your bloody wanderings. Why can't you stay where you were born, like everybody else?'

''Cos I'm not like everybody else. And *they're* not going to make me.'

'You want to button your lip, talking like that. Or *they'll* hear you.'

'Or *you'll* tell them.' Then Martin saw the look on his father's face and was sorry. The old man would never do a thing like that. Not like some fathers . . .

He was still staring at the card offering the vacancy when a
blond kid came out, and spat on the pavement with a lot of
feeling.

'Been havin' a go?' asked Martin mildly.

'It's a con,' said the kid. 'They set you an intelligence test that
would sink the Prime Minister.' He was no slouch or lout,
either. Still held himself upright; switched-on blue eyes. Another
lost sixth-former. 'Waste of time!'

'I don't know . . .' said Martin. In school, he'd been rather
sharp on intelligence tests.

'Suit yourself,' said the blond kid, and walked away.

Martin still hesitated. Then it started to rain, spattering his
thin jeans. That settled it. The grey afternoon looked so pointless
that even failing an intelligence sounded a big thrill. Sometimes
they gave you coffee . . .

He walked in; the woman sitting knitting looked up, bored,
plump and ginger. Pale blue eyes swam behind her spectacles
like timid tropical fish.

'What's the vacancy?'

'Oh . . .just a general vacancy. Want to apply?'

He shrugged. 'Why not?' She passed him a ballpoint and a
many-paged green intelligence test.

'Ready?' She clicked a stopwatch into action, and put it on
the desk in front of her, as if she'd done it a million times before.
'Forty minutes.' He sighed with satisfaction as his ballpoint
sliced into the test. It was like biting a ham sandwich, like
coming home.

An hour later, she was pushing back agitated wisps of ginger
hair and speaking into the office intercom, her voice a squeak of
excitement, a near-mad glint in her blue tropical-fish eyes.

'Mr Boston — I've just tested a young man — a very high
score — a very high score indeed. Highest score in *months*.'

'Contain yourself, Miss Feather. What is the score?' It was a
deliberately dull voice that not only killed her excitement dead
as a falling pigeon, but made her pull down her plaid skirt,
already well below her knees.

'Four hundred and ninety-eight, Mr Boston.'

Might be worth giving him a PA 52. Yes, try him with a PA

52. We've nothing better to do this afternoon.'

PA 52 was twice as thick as the other one. As Martin took it, a little warm shiver trickled down his spine. Gratitude? To *them*? For what? Not rejecting him outright, like the blond kid? He smashed down the gratitude with a heavy mental fist; they'd only fail him further on. They were just playing with him. They had no job; there were no jobs. Still, he might as well get something out of his moment of triumph.

'Could I have a cup of coffee? Before I start?'

'Oh, I think we could manage a cup of coffee. You start, and I'll put it by your elbow when it's ready.' She clucked around him like she was an old mother hen, and he the only egg she'd ever laid. Smoothly, with a sense of ascending power, he began to cut through PA 52.

'Sit down,' said Mr Boston, steepling long nicotined fingers. He consulted PA 52 slyly, slantingly. 'Erm . . . Martin, isn't it?'

'Mmmm,' said Martin. He thought that Boston, with his near-religious air of relaxed guilt and pinstripe brown suit (shiny at cuff and elbow, and no doubt backside, if backside had been visible) was more like a careers officer than any employer. Employers were much better dressed, ran frantic fingers through their hair, and expected to answer the phone any minute. Still, he'd only met two employers in his life; they'd turned him down before he left school.

'I see you're interested in working with people?'

'Oh, yes, *very*,' said Martin, outwardly eager, inwardly mocking. You were taught in first-year always to say you were terribly keen on people. Jobs with machinery no longer existed; only computers talked to computers now.

'I see leadership potential here.' Boston peered into PA 52 like it was a crystal-ball. 'A lot of leadership. Do you find it easy to persuade others . . . your friends . . . to do what *you* want?'

'Oh yes.' Martin thought of the copies of his underground-newspaper, rolled up and pushed down the hollow tubes of his bike, ready for distribution to the various districts. Getting the newspaper team together had taken a lot of persuasion. Persuading pretty little girls to be the news-gatherers, which meant sleeping with grubby elderly civil servants for the sake of their pillowtalk. Getting the printers, with their old hand-operated cyclostyling machine, set up in a makeshift hut in the middle of Rubbishtip 379, after the spy-cameras, sprayed daily with salt-water, had rusted solid and stood helpless as stuffed birds. 'Yes, I find it easy to persuade others to do what I want.'

'*Good*,' said Mr Boston. He leaned forward to his intercom. 'Miss Feather — bring our friend Martin here another cup of coffee — the continental blend this time, I think.' Somewhere in the small terraced building, a large electrical machine began to hum, slightly but not unpleasantly vibrating the old walls. Some percolator, Martin thought, with a slight smile. He was already starting to feel proprietorial, patronising about this old dump.

Boston re-steepled his fingers, and slantingly consulted PA 52 again. 'And bags of initiative . . . you're a good long way from home, here. Five whole districts. Have you walked? You must be fit.'

'I've got an old bicycle . . .'

'A bike? Bless my soul.' So great was Boston's surprise that he took off his spectacles, folded their arms neatly across each other, and popped them into the breast-pocket of his suit. He surveyed Martin with naked eyes, candid, weary and brown-edged as an old dog's. 'I haven't seen a bike in years, though I did my share of riding as a boy. Where did you find this bike?'

'At the metal-eater. Had to build it up from bits.'

Mr Boston's excitement was now so great that he had to put his spectacles on again. 'Yes, yes, your mechanical aptitude and manual dexterity show up here on PA 52. And your patience. But . . .' and his voice fell like the Tellypreacher's when he came to the Sins of the Flesh, 'it wasn't awfully honest, was it, taking that bike away from the metal-eater? It already belonged to the State . . .'

Martin's heart sank. This was the point where the job interview fell apart. Even before he got his second cup of coffee. It had been going so well . . . but he knew better than to try to paper over the cracks. He hardened his heart and got up.

'Stuff the State,' he said, watching Boston's eyes for the expression of shock that would be the last pay-off of this whole lousy business.

But Boston didn't look shocked. He took off his spectacles

and waved them; a look of boyish glee suffused his face.

'Stuff the State . . . exactly. Well, not exactly . . .' he corrected himself with an effort. 'We all depend upon the State, but we know it isn't omniscient. To the mender of washing-machines, the State supplies split-pins at a reasonable price, within a reasonable time. But suppose our supply of split-pins has run out already, because we imprudently neglected to reorder in time? We still want our split-pins *now* — even if we have to pay twice the legal price. That is my . . . our . . . little business. Greasing the wheels of state, as I always tell my wife (who is a director of our little firm).' He polished his spectacles enthusiastically with a little stained brown cloth, taken from his spectacle case for the purpose.

'And if we get caught?' asked Martin; but his mood soared.

'A heavy fine . . . the firm will pay. Or a short prison sentence; that soon passes. We're commercial criminals, not political. We do not wish to overthrow the State, only oil its wheels, oil its wheels. The State understands this.'

They eyed each other. Martin still thought Boston didn't talk like a businessman. But the chances this firm offered . . . His own bedsitter, perhaps a firm's van . . . better still, a chance to smuggle on his own behalf. Not just paper for the newspaper . . . perhaps high-grade steel tubing for guns. He looked at Boston doubtfully; jobs just didn't grow on trees like this. Boston licked his lips, almost pleading, like an old spaniel.

'Sounds a good doss,' said Martin doubtfully.

'Then you accept the vacancy?' You're a most suitable candidate.'

Miss Feather came in with the second cup of coffee.

'Will there be a chance to travel?' asked Martin.

'Almost immediately,' said Mr Boston, and Miss Feather nodded in smiling agreement. 'We will have to process you now. Would you mind waiting in here?'

The waiting room was tiny. Just enough room for a bentwood chair, and a toffee-varnished rack containing a few worn copies of the State magazine at the very end of their life. Martin was surprised anybody had ever bothered to read them; everyone knew they were all glossy lies. There was a strange selection of posters on the walls — Fight Tooth Decay, an advert for the

local museum of industrial sewing machines, and a travel poster
featuring an unknown tropical island. Martin wondered if his
new job would take him anywhere near there. His head was
whirling with the strange drunkenness of accepting and being
accepted. Blood pounded all over his body. The vibrations of
that damned machine were coming through the waiting room
walls, and going right through his head. It sounded a clapped-
out machine, as if it was trying but would never make it.

Too late, the tiny size of the waiting room warned him; the
oppressive warmth. He pulled at the closed door, but it had no
handle this side. He hammered on it; heavy metal.

Then there was a crack of blue darkness inside his head.
When he opened his eyes again, he was standing in a room
exactly the same size, but walled with stainles steel and excruci-
atingly cold. He shivered, but not just with cold.

There was a great round window set in the door. In the
window floated the moon, only it was too big, pale blue and
green, scarfed in a white that could only be clouds. Below were
low white hills like ash-tips. Nearer, lying on the ashy soil, what
looked like heaps of the stringy frozen chops you found in the
deep-freeze of the most wretched supermarkets. From among
the heaps, white skulls watched him, patiently waiting.

But much worse was the black sky, the totally black sky. In
which stars glowed huge and incandescent, red, blue, yellow,
orange. Some pulsed, at varying rhythms; others shone steadily.

'There!' Boston's voice came from a grille above the door,
crackly with radio-static. 'There's your vacancy, Martin. Outer
space. The biggest vacancy there is!' His voice was almost
gentle, almost proud, almost pleading. 'Look your fill — I can
only give you another minute.'

Quite unable to think of anything else to do, Martin continued
to gaze at the pulsing stars. Then the door of the capsule slid
aside. His body, sucked outwards by the vacuum, turning
slowly in the low gravity, exploded in half-a-dozen places in
rapid succession. The force of the explosions shot out great
clouds of red vapour, that sank swiftly to the surface of the
white ash. Continuing explosions drove his disintegrating body
across the mounds of his predecessors like an erratic fire-cracker.
Then, indistinguishable from the rest of the heaps, except for its

fresh redness, it settled to the freeze-drying, vacuum-drying of total vacancy.

'It always seems to me a pity,' said Mr Boston, 'that anything as wonderful as the Moon Teleport should have been reduced to *this* use. We could have conquered space, if we'd only discovered how to bring people *back*. Now it's no more than a garbage-disposal unit.'

'I always feel so flat afterwards,' said Miss Feather. She lifted a faded print of Constable's *Haywain* from the wall, revealing a row of stainless-steel buttons and a digital read-out in green.

11,075,019

She tapped the buttons rapidly. The number went down one.

11,075,018

Then resumed its inexorable climb.

11,075,019
11,075,020

Miss Feather gave a slight shudder of distaste, and replaced *The Haywain*.

'Pity we can't send them all that way.' She pressed her hairstyle back into place with the aid of her compact mirror.

'Do you know how much it costs to send *one* to the moon? asked Boston. 'No, we can only send the dangerous ones. The ones that qualify for the vacancy.'

'*Was* he dangerous?'

'He might have become so. Intelligence, leadership, initiative, mobility, ingenuity, curiosity — all the warning signs were there. It doesn't pay to be sentimental, Miss Feather — I believe young tiger cubs are quite cuddleable in their first weeks of life. Nevertheless, they become tigers. We remove the tiger cubs so that the rest, the sheep, may safely graze, as one might put it. I only fear we might not catch enough tiger cubs in time. The young keep on coming like an inexorable flood, wanting what their fathers and grandfathers had. They could sweep us away.'

They sat looking at each other, in mildly depressed silence.

'That bicycle was a sure sign,' said Boston at last. 'Most original — first I've seen in years. Originality is always a danger. I'd better get the bike off the street, before it's noticed. Ring the metal-eater people, will you?'

Miss Feather rang; put the kettle on for another cup of coffee.
Mr Boston came back empty-handed, perturbed.

'It's gone. Someone's taken it.'

'A sneak-thief?'

'Then he's a very stupid sneak-thief,' said Boston savagely.
'Stealing a unique object he'd never dare ride in public.'

'You don't think one of his friends . . . should we ring for the
police?' Her hand went to the necklace round her throat,
nervously.

'To report the theft of a bicycle that didn't belong to us in the
first place? They'd think that pretty irregular. They'd want to
know where our young friend Martin had got to . . .'

'Shall we ring the Ministry?'

'My dear Miss Feather, they'd think we were losing our
nerve. You don't fancy premature retirement, do you?'

She paled. He nodded, satisfied. 'Then I think we'd better just
sit it out.'

Facing each other with a growing silent unease, as the light
faded in the grubby street outside, they settled down to wait.

Personal Essay
by Robert Westall

Writing a short story is different from writing a novel. Novels grow slowly in your mind, with a longer gestation period than elephants have. It takes two years to produce a baby elephant; my novel *Futuretrack Five* was conceived in the summer of 1977, and not published until 1983. Novels grow in my mind like thunderstorms — the clouds of tension build up, there is an occasional flash of lightning when a character comes to birth, but all is a murky whirling chaos in which plots, characters and events change again and again. But always I can feel the storm coming on; I know it is going to rain eventually.

I have even been in the state where three novels were struggling with each other in my mind, each trying to get born at the same time. (*The Devil on the Road*, *Scarecrows* and *The Cats of Seroster*.) *The Devil* won, drove the others into the background and got born first. When a novel is about to arrive I get broody and self-protective, even selfish. I avoid taking on other commitments. Luckily a novel takes only about four weeks to actually *write*, so I get forgiven and am admitted back to the human race afterwards. I need a reassurance of personal peace, even boredom, in my outside life, before I can start a novel.

On the other hand, I can write a short story any time, even in times of intense personal misery, and they just come out the more powerful for the misery. As Hemingway advised Scott Fitzgerald, squeeze your suffering into the story; make it work for you. 'Break of Dark', was written in the darkest hours of my life so far; I could not have written it in a happy time.

Short story plots leap into my mind instantly, when I am busy teaching or just walking along. I don't feel them coming, but usually they come when I've just been commissioned to write one, which is commercially convenient. Whereas I couldn't bear to have a novel *commissioned*. I write it in secret, like Moses going up into the mountain alone, return with it as if it were the tablets of stone, and try to flog it to one of my three publishers who don't even know it's coming.

Normally a short story begins with the question 'What if?' 'What if astronauts discovered the moon was really made of green cheese; what would the commercial implications be? What if I came home one night, and found the front door swinging open, the house dark and my wife missing?'

Mind you, I've twice had stories that became both short stories and novels. One was 'Urn Burial', about a boy who discovers a space-warrior buried with his weapons. In the story, the tomb auto-destructs, giving one ending; in the novel the tomb doesn't auto-destruct, giving another, much longer ending. 'The Vacancy' is similarly one of a pair from the same idea. The novel was *Futuretrack Five*. Both concern the question 'What if the government, unable to find jobs for the young, sets out to solve the problem by destroying the young?' It deals with the alarming idea of a criminal, psychopathic government. All governments are criminal, to a great or slight degree.

'The Vacancy' was written midway through my writing of *Futuretrack Five*. I suppose I was putting my toe in the water, to see what public reaction would be to my ideas of governmental criminal activity against the young. I felt very tense at the time, because I was the Head of Careers in a sixth-form college, and had up until then been very efficient at finding jobs for my students; we had a careers team of thirteen teachers, and the students got a careers interview on request, the same day. It was working beautifully, until the morning when the recruiting officer of ERF lorries rang up to cancel ten apprenticeships my boys had earned by hard interview. The man was in tears; we both felt we had betrayed the young in a dreadful way; it affected me worse than the beginning of World War II when I was a boy.

It made me feel that the young, as far as the state was concerned, were expendable. We had cared for them, fed and educated them better than any previous generation, and now they were to be ruthlessly thrown on the rubbish-tip, never used. It reminded me of the Somme during the first World War; it reminded me of the prolific and ruthless waste of young salmon, who are spawned, millions from one mother-fish, in the hope that *one* will survive predators and reach maturity. The basic ruthlessness of life oppressed me.

The story crystallised on an Easter holiday in Anglesey. We had parked in one of the back streets of Menai Bridge, a dull boring brown little street; in one of the windows of the identical houses was a sign merely saying 'Vacancy'. My mind played about with the two meanings of 'Vacancy', and the whole story was sitting in my head within thirty seconds. When I got home, I wrote it straight through, without hesitating once. I felt rage when I wrote it, because any selection process is a humiliating mincing-machine. I hated selection procedures and the damage they did, even when there were plenty of jobs and the boy got the one he wanted. He sold his soul to the devil and got a good price . . . now, children would similarly sell their souls to the devil and be offered . . . vacancy.

Martin in 'The Vacancy' is the twin-brother of Henry Kitson in *Futuretrack Five*. Both are intelligent, adaptable, switched-on and full of initiative. Martin loses at an early stage in his battle against the state, so it's a short story; Henry Kitson lasts longer, and gains a sort of victory and revenge, so it's a novel. But Henry suffers a far deeper disillusionment than Martin — it's hard to know who to envy least.

RICHARD CONNELL

The Most Dangerous Game

'Off there to the right — somewhere — is a large island,' said Whitney. 'It's rather a mystery—'

'What island is it?' Rainsford asked.'

'The old charts call it "Ship-Trap Island,"' Whitney replied. 'A suggestive name, isn't it? Sailors have a curious dread of the place. I don't know why. Some superstition—'

'Can't see it,' remarked Rainsford, trying to peer through the dank tropical night that was palpable as it pressed its thick warm blackness in upon the yacht.

'You've good eyes,' said Whitney, with a laugh, 'and I've seen you pick off a moose moving in the brown fall bush at four hundred yards, but even you can't see four miles or so through a moonless Caribbean night.'

'Not four yards,' admitted Rainsford. 'Ugh! It's like moist black velvet.'

'It will be light enough in Rio,' promised Whitney. 'We should make it in a few days. I hope the jaguar guns have come from Purdey's. We should have some good hunting up the Amazon. Great sport, hunting.'

'The best sport in the world,' agreed Rainsford.

'For the hunter,' amended Whitney. 'Not for the jaguar.'

'Don't talk rot, Whitney,' said Rainsford. 'You're a big-game hunter, not a philosopher. Who cares how a jaguar feels?'

'Perhaps the jaguar does,' observed Whitney.

'Bah! They've no understanding.'

'Even so, I rather think they understand one thing — fear. The fear of pain and the fear of death.'

'Nonsense,' laughed Rainsford. 'This hot weather is making you soft, Whitney. Be a realist. The world is made up of two classes — the hunters and the hunted. Luckily, you and I are hunters. Do you think we've passed that island yet?'

'I can't tell in the dark. I hope so.'

'Why?' asked Rainsford.

'The place has a reputation — a bad one.'

'Cannibals?' suggested Rainsford.

'Hardly. Even cannibals wouldn't live in such a God-forsaken place. But it's gotten into sailor lore, somehow. Didn't you notice that the crew's nerves seemed a bit jumpy today?'

'They were a bit strange, now you mention it. Even Captain Nielsen—'

'Yes, even that tough-minded old Swede, who'd go up to the devil himself and ask him for a light. Those fishy blue eyes held a look I never saw there before. All I could get out of him was: "This place has an evil name among seafaring men, sir." Then he said to me, very gravely: "Don't you feel anything?" — as if the air about us was actually poisonous. Now, you mustn't laugh when I tell you this — I did feel something like a sudden chill.

'There was no breeze. The sea was as flat as a plate-glass window. We were drawing near the island then. What I felt was a — mental chill; a sort of sudden dread.'

'Pure imagination,' said Rainsford. 'One superstitious sailor can taint the whole ship's company with his fear.'

'Maybe. But sometimes I think sailors have an extra sense that tells them when they are in danger. Sometimes I think evil is a tangible thing — with wave lengths, just as sound and light have. An evil place can, so to speak, broadcast vibrations of evil. Anyhow, I'm glad we're getting out of this zone. Well, I think I'll turn in now, Rainsford.'

'I'm not sleepy,' said Rainsford. 'I'm going to smoke another pipe up on the afterdeck.'

'Good night, then, Rainsford. See you at breakfast.'

'Right. Good night, Whitney.'

There was no sound in the night as Rainsford sat there, but the muffled throb of the engine that drove the yacht swiftly through the darkness, and the swish and ripple of the wash of the propeller.

Rainsford, reclining in a steamer chair, indolently puffed on his favourite briar. The sensuous drowsiness of the night was on him. 'It's so dark,' he thought, 'that I could sleep without closing my eyes; the night would be my eyelids—'

An abrupt sound startled him. Off to the right he heard it, and his ears, expert in such matters, could not be mistaken. Again he heard the sound, and again. Somewhere, off in the blackness, someone had fired a gun three times.

Rainsford sprang up and moved quickly to the rail, mystified. He strained his eyes in the direction from which the reports had come, but it was like trying to see through a blanket. He leaped upon the rail and balanced himself there, to get greater elevation; his pipe, striking a rope, was knocked from his mouth. He lunged for it; a short, hoarse cry came from his lips as he realised he had reached too far and had lost his balance. The cry was pinched off short as the blood-warm waters of the Caribbean Sea closed over his head.

He struggled up to the surface and tried to cry out, but the wash from the speeding yacht slapped him in the face and the salt water in his open mouth made him gag and strangle. Desperately he struck out with strong strokes after the receding lights of the yacht, but he stopped before he had swum fifty feet. A certain coolheadedness had come to him; it was not the first time he had been in a tight place. There was a chance that his cries could be heard by someone aboard the yacht, but that chance was slender, and grew more slender as the yacht raced on. He wrestled himself out of his clothes, and shouted with all his power. The lights of the yacht became faint and ever-vanishing fireflies; then they were blotted out entirely by the night.

Rainsford remembered the shots. They had come from the right, and doggedly he swam in that direction, swimming with slow, deliberate strokes, conserving his strength. For a seemingly endless time he fought the sea. He began to count his strokes; he could do possibly a hundred more and then—

Rainsford heard a sound. It came out of the darkness, a high, screaming sound, the sound of an animal in an extremity of anguish and terror.

He did not recognise the animal that made the sound; he did not try to; with fresh vitality he swam toward the sound. He heard it again; then it was cut short by another noise, crisp, staccato.

'Pistol shot,' muttered Rainsford, swimming on.

Ten minutes of determined effort brought another sound to his ears — the most welcome he had ever heard — the muttering and growling of the sea breaking on a rocky shore. He was almost on the rocks before he saw them; on a night less calm he would have been shattered against them. With his remaining strength he dragged himself from the swirling waters. Jagged crags appeared to jut up into the opaqueness; he forced himself upward, hand over hand. Gasping, his hands raw, he reached a flat place at the top. Dense jungle came down to the very edge of the cliffs. What perils that tangle of trees and underbrush might hold for him did not concern Rainsford just then. All he knew was that he was safe from his enemy, the sea, and that utter weariness was on him. He flung himself down at the jungle edge and tumbled headlong into the deepest sleep of his life.

When he opened his eyes he knew from the position of the sun that it was late in the afternoon. Sleep had given him new vigour; a sharp hunger was picking at him. He looked about him, almost cheerfully.

'Where there are pistol shots, there are men. Where there are men, there is food,' he thought. But what kind of men, he wondered, in so forbidding a place? An unbroken front of snarled and ragged jungle fringed the shore.

He saw no sign of a trail through the closely knit web of weeds and trees; it was easier to go along the shore, and Rainsford floundered along by the water. Not far from where he had landed, he stopped.

Some wounded thing, by the evidence a large animal, had thrashed about in the underbrush; the jungle weeds were crushed down and the moss was lacerated; one patch of weeds was stained crimson. A small, glittering object not far away caught

Rainsford's eye and he picked it up. It was an empty cartridge.

'A twenty-two,' he remarked. 'That's odd. It must have been a fairly large animal too. The hunter had his nerve with him to tackle it with a light gun. It's clear that the brute put up a fight. I suppose the first three shots I heard was when the hunter flushed his quarry and wounded it. The last shot was when he trailed it here and finished it.'

He examined the ground closely and found what he had hoped to find — the print of hunting-boots. They pointed along the cliff in the direction he had been going. Eagerly he hurried along, now slipping on a rotten log or a loose stone, but making headway; night was beginning to settle down on the island.

Bleak darkness was blacking out the sea and jungle when Rainsford sighted the lights. He came upon them as he turned a crook in the coast line, and his first thought was that he had come upon a village, for there were many lights. But as he forged along he saw to his great astonishment that all the lights were in one enormous building — a lofty structure with pointed towers plunging upward into the gloom. His eyes made out the shadowy outlines of a palatial château; it was set on a high bluff, and on three sides of it cliffs dived down to where the sea licked greedy lips in the shadows.

'Mirage,' thought Rainsford. But it was no mirage, he found, when he opened the tall spiked iron gate. The stone steps were real enough; the massive door with a leering gargoyle for a knocker was real enough; yet about it all hung an air of unreality.

He lifted the knocker, and it creaked up stiffly, as if it had never before been used. He let it fall, and it startled him with its booming loudness. He thought he heard steps within; the door remained closed. Again Rainsford lifted the heavy knocker, and let it fall. The door opened then, opened as suddenly as if it were on a spring, and Rainsford stood blinking in the river of glaring gold light that poured out. The first thing Rainsford's eyes discerned was the largest man Rainsford had ever seen — a gigantic creature, solidly made and black-bearded to the waist. In his hand the man held a long-barrelled revolver, and he was pointing it straight at Rainsford's heart.

Out of the snarl of beard two small eyes regarded Rainsford.

'Don't be alarmed,' said Rainsford, with a smile which he hoped was disarming. 'I'm no robber. I fell off a yacht. My name is Sanger Rainsford of New York City.'

The menacing look in the eyes did not change. The revolver pointed as rigidly as if the giant were a statue. He gave no sign that he understood Rainsford's words, or that he had even heard them. He was dressed in uniform, a black uniform trimmed with grey astrakhan.

'I'm Sanger Rainsford of New York,' Rainsford began again. 'I fell off a yacht. I am hungry.'

The man's only answer was to raise with his thumb the hammer of his revolver. Then Rainsford saw the man's free hand go to his forehead in a military salute, and he saw him click his heels together and stand at attention. Another man was coming down the broad marble steps, an erect, slender man in evening clothes. He advanced to Rainsford and held out his hand.

In a cultivated voice marked by a slight accent that gave it added precision and deliberateness, he said: 'It is a very great pleasure and honour to welcome Mr Sanger Rainsford, the celebrated hunter, to my home.'

Automatically Rainsford shook the man's hand.

'I've read your book about hunting snow leopards in Tibet, you see,' explained the man. 'I am General Zaroff.'

Rainsford's first impression was that the man was singularly handsome; his second was that there was an original, almost bizarre quality about the general's face. He was a tall man past middle age, for his hair was a vivid white; but his thick eyebrows and pointed military moustache were as black as the night from which Rainsford had come. His eyes, too, were black and very bright. He had high cheekbones, a sharp-cut nose, a spare dark face, the face of a man used to giving orders, the face of an aristocrat. Turning to the giant in uniform, the general made a sign. The giant put away his pistol, saluted, withdrew.

'Ivan is an incredibly strong fellow,' remarked the general, but he has the misfortune to be deaf and dumb. A simple fellow, but, I'm afraid, like all his race, a bit of a savage.'

'Is he Russian?'

'He is a Cossack,' said the general, and his smile showed red lips and pointed teeth. 'So am I.'

'Come,' he said, 'we shouldn't be chatting here. We can talk later. Now you want clothes, food, rest. You shall have them. This is a most restful spot.'

Ivan had reappeared, and the general spoke to him with lips that moved but gave forth no sound.

'Follow Ivan, if you please, Mr Rainsford,' said the general. 'I was about to have my dinner when you came. I'll wait for you. You'll find that my clothes will fit you, I think.'

It was to a huge, beam-ceilinged bedroom with a canopied bed big enough for six men that Rainsford followed the silent giant. Ivan laid out an evening suit, and Rainsford, as he put it on, noticed that it came from a London tailor who ordinarily cut and sewed for none below the rank of duke.

The dining-room to which Ivan conducted him was in many ways remarkable. There was a medieval magnificence about it; it suggested a baronial hall of feudal times with its oaken panels, its high ceiling, its vast refectory table where twoscore men could sit down to eat. About the hall were the mounted heads of many animals — lions, tigers, elephants, moose, bears; larger or more perfect specimens Rainsford had never seen. At the great table the general was sitting alone.

'You'll have a cocktail, Mr Rainsford,' he suggested. The cocktail was surpassingly good; and, Rainsford noted, the table appointments were of the finest — the linen, the crystal, the silver, the china.

They were eating *borsch*, the rich, red soup with whipped cream so dear to Russian palates. Half apologetically General Zaroff said: 'We do our best to preserve the amenities of civilisation here. Please forgive any lapses. We are well off the beaten track, you know. Do you think the champagne has suffered from its long ocean trip?'

'Not in the least,' declared Rainsford. He was finding the general a most thoughtful and affable host, a true cosmopolite. But there was one small trait of the general's that made Rainsford uncomfortable. Whenever he looked up from his plate he found the general studying him, appraising him narrowly.

'Perhaps,' said General Zaroff, 'you were surprised that I

recognised your name. You see, I read all books on hunting published in English, French, and Russian. I have but one passion in my life, Mr Rainsford, and it is the hunt.'

'You have some wonderful heads here,' said Rainsford as he ate a particularly well-cooked *filet mignon*. 'That Cape buffalo is the largest I ever saw.'

'Oh, that fellow. Yes, he was a monster.'

'Did he charge you?'

'Hurled me against a tree,' said the general. 'Fractured my skull. But I got the brute.'

'I've always thought,' said Rainsford, 'that the Cape buffalo is the most dangerous of all big game.'

For a moment the general did not reply; he was smiling his curious red-lipped smile. Then he said slowly: 'No. You are wrong, sir. The Cape buffalo is not the most dangerous big game.' He sipped his wine. 'Here in my preserve on this island,' he said in the same slow tone, 'I hunt more dangerous game.'

Rainsford expressed his surprise. 'Is there big game on this island?'

The general nodded. 'The biggest.'

'Really?'

'Oh, it isn't here naturally, of course. I have to stock the island.'

'What have you imported, general?' Rainsford asked. 'Tigers?'

The general smiled. 'No,' he said. 'Hunting tigers ceased to interest me some years ago. I exhausted their possibilities, you see. No thrill left in tigers, no real danger. I live for danger, Mr Rainsford.'

The general took from his pocket a gold cigarette-case and offered his guest a long black cigarette with a silver tip; it was perfumed and gave off a smell like incense.

'We will have some capital hunting, you and I,' said the general. 'I shall be most glad to have your society.'

'But what game—' began Rainsford.

'I'll tell you,' said the general. 'You will be amused, I know. I think I may say, in all modesty, that I have done a rare thing. I have invented a new sensation. May I pour you another glass of port, Mr Rainsford?'

'Thank you, general.'

The general filled both glasses, and said: 'God makes some men poets. Some He makes kings, some beggars. Me He made a hunter. My hand was made for the trigger, my father said. He was a very rich man with a quarter of a million acres in the Crimea, and he was an ardent sportsman. When I was only five years old he gave me a little gun, specially made in Moscow for me, to shoot sparrows with. When I shot some of his prize turkeys with it, he did not punish me; he complimented me on my marksmanship. I killed my first bear in the Caucasus when I was ten. My whole life has been one prolonged hunt. I went into the army — it was expected of noblemen's sons — and for a time commanded a division of Cossack cavalry, but my real interest was always the hunt. I have hunted every kind of game in every land. It would be impossible for me to tell you how many animals I have killed.'

The general puffed at his cigarette.

'After the débâcle in Russia I left the country, for it was imprudent of an officer of the Czar to stay there. Many noble Russians lost everything. I, luckily, had invested heavily in American securities, so I shall never have to open a tearoom in Monte Carlo or drive a taxi in Paris. Naturally, I continued to hunt — grizzlies in your Rockies, crocodiles in the Ganges, rhinoceroses in East Africa. It was in Africa that the Cape buffalo hit me and laid me up for six months. As soon as I recovered I started for the Amazon to hunt jaguars, for I had heard they were unusually cunning. They weren't.' The Cossack sighed. 'They were no match at all for a hunter with his wits about him, and a high-powered rifle. I was bitterly disappointed. I was lying in my tent with a splitting headache one night when a terrible thought pushed its way into my mind. Hunting was beginning to bore me! And hunting, remember, had been my life. I have heard that in America businessmen often go to pieces when they give up the business that has been their life.'

'Yes, that's so,' said Rainsford.

The general smiled. 'I had no wish to go to pieces,' he said. 'I must do something. Now, mine is an analytical mind, Mr Rainsford. Doubtless that is why I enjoy the problems of the chase.'

'No doubt, General Zaroff.'

'So,' continued the general, 'I asked myself why the hunt no longer fascinated me. You are much younger than I am, Mr Rainsford, and have not hunted as much, but you perhaps can guess the answer.'

'What was it?'

'Simply this: hunting had ceased to be what you call "a sporting proposition". It had become too easy. I always got my quarry. Always. There is no greater bore than perfection.'

The general lit a fresh cigarette.

'No animal had a chance with me any more. That is no boast; it is a mathematical certainty. The animal had nothing but his legs and his instinct. Instinct is no match for reason. When I thought of this it was a tragic moment for me, I can tell you.'

Rainsford leaned across the table, absorbed in what his host was saying.

'It came to me as an inspiration what I must do,' the general went on.

'And that was?'

The general smiled the quiet smile of one who has faced an obstacle and surmounted it with success. 'I had to invent a new animal to hunt,' he said.

'A new animal? You're joking.'

'Not at all,' said the general. 'I never joke about hunting. I needed a new animal. I found one. So I bought this island, built this house, and here I do my hunting. The island is perfect for my purposes — there are jungles with a maze of trails in them, hills, swamps—'

'But the animal, General Zaroff?'

'Oh,' said the general, 'it supplies me with the most exciting hunting in the world. No other hunting compares with it for an instant. Every day I hunt, and I never grow bored now, for I have a quarry with which I can match my wits.'

Rainsford's bewilderment showed in his face.

'I wanted the ideal animal to hunt,' explained the general. 'So I said: "What are the attributes of an ideal quarry?" And the answer was, of course: "It must have courage, cunning, and, above all, it must be able to reason."'

'But no animal can reason,' objected Rainsford.

'My dear fellow,' said the general, 'there is one that can.'

'But you can't mean—' gasped Rainsford.

'And why not?'

'I can't believe you are serious, General Zaroff. This is a grisly joke.'

'Why should I not be serious? I am speaking of hunting.'

'Hunting? Good God, General Zaroff, what you speak of is murder.'

The general laughed with entire good nature. He regarded Rainsford quizzically. 'I refuse to believe that so modern and civilised a young man as you seem to be harbours romantic ideas about the value of human life. Surely your experiences in the war—'

'Did not make me condone cold-blooded murder,' finished Rainsford stiffly.

Laughter shook the general. 'How extraordinarily droll you are!' he said. 'One does not expect nowadays to find a young man of the educated class, even in America, with such a naïve, and, if I may say so, mid-Victorian point of view. It's like finding a snuffbox in a limousine. Ah, well, doubtless you had Puritan ancestors. So many Americans appear to have had. I'll wager you'll forget your notions when you go hunting with me. You've a genuine new thrill in store for you, Mr Rainsford.'

'Thank you, I'm a hunter, not a murderer.'

'Dear me,' said the general, quite unruffled, 'again that unpleasant word. But I think I can show you that your scruples are quite ill-founded.'

'Yes?'

'Life is for the strong, to be lived by the strong, and, if needs be, taken by the strong. The weak of the world were put here to give the strong pleasure. I am strong. Why should I not use my gift? If I wish to hunt, why should I not? I hunt the scum of the earth — a thoroughbred horse or hound is worth more than a score of them.'

'But they are men,' said Rainsford hotly.

'Precisely,' said the general. 'That is why I use them. It gives me pleasure. They can reason, after a fashion. So they are dangerous.'

'But where do you get them?'

The general's left eyelid fluttered down in a wink. 'This island is called "Ship-Trap",' he answered. 'Sometimes an angry god of the high seas sends them to me. Sometimes, when Providence is not so kind, I help Providence a bit. Come to the window with me.'

Rainsford went to the window and looked out toward the sea.

'Watch! Out there!' exclaimed the general, pointing into the night. Rainsford's eyes saw only blackness, and then, as the general pressed a button, far out to sea Rainsford saw the flash of lights.

The general chuckled. 'They indicate a channel,' he said, 'where there's none: giant rocks with razor edges crouch like a sea monster with wide-open jaws. They can crush a ship as easily as I crush this nut.' He dropped a walnut on the hardwood floor and brought his heel grinding down on it. 'Oh, yes,' he said, casually, as if in answer to a question, 'I have electricity. We try to be civilised here.'

'Civilised? And you shoot down men?'

A trace of anger was in the general's black eyes, but it was there for but a second, and he said, in his most pleasant manner: 'Dear me, what a righteous young man you are! I assure you I do not do the thing you suggest. That would be barbarous. I treat these visitors with every consideration. They get plenty of good food and exercise. They get into splendid physical condition. You shall see for yourself tomorrow.'

'What do you mean?'

'We'll visit my training school,' smiled the general. 'It's in the cellar. I have about a dozen pupils down there now. They're from the Spanish bark *San Lucar* that had the bad luck to go on the rocks out there. A very inferior lot, I regret to say. Poor specimens and more accustomed to the deck than to the jungle.'

He raised his hand, and Ivan, who served as waiter, brought thick Turkish coffee. Rainsford, with an effort, held his tongue in check.

'It's a game, you see,' pursued the general blandly. 'I suggest to one of them that we go hunting. I give him a supply of food and an excellent hunting knife. I give him three hours' start. I am to follow, armed only with a pistol of the smallest calibre and range. If my quarry eludes me for three whole days, he wins the game. If I find him' — the general smiled — 'he loses.'

'Suppose he refuses to be hunted?'

'Oh,' said the general, 'I give him his option, of course. He need not play that game if he doesn't wish to. If he does not wish to hunt, I turn him over to Ivan. Ivan once had the honour of serving as official knouter to the Great White Czar, and he has his own ideas of sport. Invariably, Mr Rainsford, invariably they choose the hunt.'

'And if they win?'

The smile on the general's face widened. 'To date I have not lost,' he said.

Then he added, hastily: 'I don't wish you to think me a braggart, Mr Rainsford. Many of them afford only the most elementary sort of problem. Occasionally I strike a Tartar. One almost did win. I eventually had to use the dogs.'

'The dogs?'

'This way, please. I'll show you.'

The general steered Rainsford to a window. The lights from the windows sent a flickering illumination that made grotesque patterns on the courtyard below, and Rainsford could see moving about there a dozen or so huge black shapes; as they turned toward him, their eyes glittered greenly.

'A rather good lot, I think,' observed the general. 'They are let out at seven every night. If anyone should try to get into my house — or out of it — something extremely regrettable would occur to him.' He hummed a snatch of song from the Folies Bergère.

'And now,' said the general, 'I want to show you my new collection of heads. Will you come with me to the library?'

'I hope,' said Rainsford, 'that you will excuse me tonight, General Zaroff. I'm really not feeling at all well.'

'Ah, indeed?' the general inquired solicitously. 'Well, I suppose that's only natural, after your long swim. You need a good, restful night's sleep. Tomorrow you'll feel like a new man, I'll wager. Then we'll hunt, eh? I've one rather promising prospect—'

Rainsford was hurrying from the room.

'Sorry you can't go with me tonight,' called the general. 'I expect rather fair sport. Well, good night, Mr Rainsford; I hope you have a good night's rest.'

The bed was good, and the pyjamas of the softest silk, and he was tired in every fibre of his being, but nevertheless Rainsford could not quiet his brain with the opiate of sleep. He lay, eyes wide open. Once he thought he heard stealthy steps in the corridor outside his room. He sought to throw open the door; it would not open. He went to the window and looked out. His room was high up in one of the towers. The lights of the château were out now, and it was dark and silent, but there was a fragment of sallow moon, and by its wan light he could see, dimly, the courtyard; there, weaving in and out in the pattern of shadow, were black, noiseless forms; the hounds heard him at the window and looked up, expectantly, with their green eyes. Rainsford went back to the bed and lay down. By many methods he tried to put himself to sleep. He had achieved a doze when, just as morning began to come, he heard, far off in the jungle, the faint report of a pistol.

General Zaroff did not appear until luncheon. He was dressed faultlessly in the tweeds of a country squire. He was solicitous about the state of Rainsford's health.

'As for me,' sighed the general, 'I do not feel so well. I am worried, Mr Rainsford. Last night I detected traces of my old complaint.'

To Rainsford's questioning glance the general said: 'Ennui. Boredom.'

Then, taking a second helping of *Crêpes Suzette*, the general explained: 'The hunting was not good last night. The fellow lost his head. He made a straight trail that offered no problems at all. That's the trouble with these sailors; they have dull brains to begin with, and they do not know how to get about in the woods. They do excessively stupid and obvious things. It's most annoying. Will you have another glass of Chablis, Mr Rainsford?'

'General,' said Rainsford firmly, 'I wish to leave this island at once.'

The general raised his thickets of eyebrows; he seemed hurt. 'But, my dear fellow,' the general protested, 'you've only just come. You've had no hunting—'

'I wish to go today,' said Rainsford. He saw the dead black eyes of the general on him, studying him. General Zaroff's face suddenly brightened.

He filled Rainsford's glass with venerable Chablis from a dusty bottle.

'Tonight,' said the general, 'we will hunt — you and I.'

Rainsford shook his head. 'No, general,' he said. 'I will not hunt.'

The general shrugged his shoulders and delicately ate a hot-house grape. 'As you wish, my friend,' he said. 'The choice rests entirely with you. But may I not venture to suggest that you will find my idea of sport more diverting than Ivan's?'

He nodded toward the corner to where the giant stood, scowling, his thick arms crossed on his hogshead of chest.

'You don't mean—' cried Rainsford.

'My dear fellow,' said the general, 'have I not told you I always mean what I say about hunting? This is really an inspiration. I drink to a foeman worthy of my steel — at last.'

The general raised his glass, but Rainsford sat staring at him. 'You'll find this game worth playing,' the general said enthusiastically. 'Your brain against mine. Your woodcraft against mine. Your strength and stamina against mine. Outdoor chess! And the stake is not without value, eh?'

'And if I win—' began Rainsford huskily.

'I'll cheerfully acknowledge myself defeated if I do not find you by midnight of the third day,' said General Zaroff. 'My sloop will place you on the mainland near a town.'

The general read what Rainsford was thinking.

'Oh, you can trust me,' said the Cossack. 'I will give you my word as a gentleman and a sportsman. Of course you, in turn, must agree to say nothing of your visit here.'

'I'll agree to nothing of the kind,' said Rainsford.

'Oh,' said the general, 'in that case — But why discuss that now? Three days hence we can discuss it over a bottle of Veuve Cliquot, unless—'

The general sipped his wine.

Then a businesslike air animated him. 'Ivan,' he said to Rainsford, 'will supply you with hunting clothes, food, a knife. I suggest you wear moccasins; they leave a poorer trail. I suggest too that you avoid the big swamp in the south-east corner of the island. We call it Death Swamp. There's quicksand there. One foolish fellow tried it. The deplorable part of it was that Lazarus followed him. You can imagine my feelings, Mr Rainsford. I loved Lazarus; he was the finest hound in my pack. Well, I must beg you to excuse me now. I always take a siesta after lunch. You'll hardly have time for a nap, I fear. You'll want to start, no doubt. I shall not follow till dusk. Hunting at night is so much more exciting than by day, don't you think? *Au revoir*, Mr Rainsford, *au revoir*.'

General Zaroff, with a deep, courtly bow, strolled from the room.

From another door came Ivan. Under one arm he carried khaki hunting clothes, a haversack of food, a leather sheath containing a long-bladed hunting knife; his right hand rested on a cocked revolver thrust in the crimson sash about his waist . . .

Rainsford had fought his way through the bush for two hours. 'I must keep my nerve. I must keep my nerve,' he said through tight teeth.

He had not been entirely clear-headed when the château gates snapped shut behind him. His whole idea at first was to put distance between himself and General Zaroff, and, to this end, he had plunged along, spurred on by the sharp rowels of something very like panic. Now he had got a grip on himself, had stopped, and was taking stock of himself and the situation.

He saw that straight flight was futile; inevitably it would bring him face to face with the sea. He was in a picture with a frame of water, and his operations, clearly, must take place within that frame.

'I'll give him a trail to follow,' muttered Rainsford, and he struck off from the rude path he had been following into the trackless wilderness. He executed a series of intricate loops; he doubled on his trail again and again, recalling all the lore of the fox hunt, and all the dodges of the fox. Night found him leg-weary, with hands and face lashed by the branches, on a thickly wooded ridge. He knew it would be insane to blunder on through the dark, even if he had the strength. His need for rest was imperative and he thought: 'I have played the fox, now I must play the cat of the fable.' A big tree with a thick trunk and outspread branches was near by, and, taking care to leave not the slightest mark, he climbed up into the crotch, and stretching out on one of the broad limbs, after a fashion, rested. Rest brought him new confidence and almost a feeling of security. Even so zealous a hunter as General Zaroff could not trace him there, he told himself; only the devil himself could follow that complicated trail through the jungle after dark. But, perhaps, the general was a devil—

An apprehensive night crawled slowly by like a wounded snake, and sleep did not visit Rainsford, although the silence of a dead world was on the jungle. Toward morning when a dingy grey was varnishing the sky, the cry of some startled bird focused Rainsford's attention in that direction. Something was coming through the bush, coming slowly, carefully, coming by the same winding way Rainsford had come. He flattened himself down on the limb, and through a screen of leaves almost as thick as tapestry, he watched. The thing that was approaching was a man.

It was General Zaroff. He made his way along with his eyes fixed in utmost concentration on the ground before him. He paused, almost beneath the tree, dropped to his knees and studied the ground. Rainsford's impulse was to hurl himself down like a panther, but he saw that the general's right hand held something metallic — a small automatic pistol.

The hunter shook his head several times, as if he were puzzled. Then he straightened up and took from his case one of his black cigarettes; its pungent incenselike smoke floated up to Rainsford's nostrils.

Rainsford held his breath. The general's eyes had left the ground and were travelling inch by inch up the tree. Rainsford froze there, every muscle tensed for a spring. But the sharp eyes of the hunter stopped before they reached the limb where Rainsford lay; a smile spread over his brown face. Very deliberately he blew a smoke ring into the air; then he turned his back on the tree and walked carelessly away, back along the trail he had come. The swish of the underbrush against his hunting-boots grew fainter and fainter.

The pent-up air burst hotly from Rainsford's lungs. His first thought made him feel sick and numb. The general could follow a trail through the woods at night; he could follow an extremely difficult trail; he must have uncanny powers; only by the merest chance had the Cossack failed to see his quarry.

Rainsford's second thought was even more terrible. It sent a shudder of cold horror through his whole being. Why had the general smiled? Why had he turned back?

Rainsford did not want to believe what his reason told him was true, but the truth was as evident as the sun that had by now pushed through the morning mists. The general was playing with him! The general was saving him for another day's sport! The Cossack was the cat; he was the mouse. Then it was that Rainsford knew the full meaning of terror.

'I will not lose my nerve. I will not.'

He slid down from the tree, and struck off again into the woods. His face was set and he forced the machinery of his mind to function. Three hundred yards from his hiding-place he stopped where a huge dead tree leaned precariously on a smaller, living one. Throwing off his sack of food, Rainsford took his knife from its sheath and began to work with all his energy.

The job was finished at last, and he threw himself down behind a fallen log a hundred feet away. He did not have to wait long. The cat was coming again to play with the mouse.

Following the trail with the sureness of a bloodhound, came General Zaroff. Nothing escaped those searching black eyes, no crushed blade of grass, no bent twig, no mark, no matter how faint, in the moss. So intent was the Cossack on his stalking that he was upon the thing Rainsford had made before he saw it. His foot touched the protruding bough that was the trigger. Even as he touched it, the general sensed his danger and leaped back with the agility of an ape. But he was not quite quick enough; the dead tree, delicately adjusted to rest on the cut living one, crashed down and struck the general a glancing blow on the shoulder as it fell; but for his alertness, he must have been smashed beneath it. He staggered, but he did not fall; nor did he drop his revolver. He stood there, rubbing his injured shoulder, and Rainsford, with fear again gripping his heart, heard the general's mocking laugh ring through the jungle.

'Rainsford,' called the general, 'if you are within sound of my voice, as I suppose you are, let me congratulate you. Not many men know how to make a Malay man-catcher. Luckily, for me, I too have hunted in Malacca. You are proving interesting, Mr

Rainsford. I am going now to have my wound dressed; it's only a slight one. But I shall be back. I shall be back.'

When the general, nursing his bruised shoulder, had gone, Rainsford took up his flight again. It was flight now, a desperate, hopeless flight, that carried him on for some hours. Dusk came, then darkness, and still he pressed on. The ground grew softer under his moccasins; the vegetation grew ranker, denser; insects bit him savagely. Then, as he stepped forward, his foot sank into the ooze. He tried to wrench it back, but the muck sucked viciously at his foot as if it were a giant leech. With a violent effort he tore his foot loose. He knew where he was now. Death Swamp and its quicksand.

His hands were tight closed as if his nerve were something tangible that someone in the darkness was trying to tear from his grip. The softness of the earth had given him an idea. He stepped back from the quicksand a dozen feet or so and, like some huge prehistoric beaver, he began to dig.

Rainsford had dug himself in in France when a second's delay meant death. That had been a placid pastime compared to his digging now. The pit grew deeper; when it was above his shoulders, he climbed out and from some hard saplings cut stakes and sharpened them to a fine point. These stakes he planted in the bottom of the pit with the points sticking up. With flying fingers he wove a rough carpet of weeds and branches and with it he covered the mouth of the pit. Then, wet with sweat and aching with tiredness, he crouched behind the stump of a lightning-charred tree.

He knew his pursuer was coming; he heard the padding sound of feet on the soft earth, and the night breeze brought him the perfume of the general's cigarette. It seemed to Rainsford that the general was coming with unusual swiftness; he was not feeling his way along, foot by foot. Rainsford, crouching there, could not see the general, nor could he see the pit. He lived a year in a minute. Then he felt an impulse to cry aloud with joy, for he heard the sharp crackle of the breaking branches as the cover of the pit gave way; he heard the sharp scream of pain as the pointed stakes found their mark. He leaped up from his place of concealment. Then he cowered back. Three feet from the pit a man was standing, with an electric torch in his hand.

'You've done well, Rainsford,' the voice of the general called. 'Your Burmese tiger pit has claimed one of my best dogs. Again you score. I think, Mr Rainsford, I'll see what you can do against my whole pack. I'm going home for a rest now. Thank you for a most amusing evening.'

At daybreak Rainsford, lying near the swamp, was awakened by a sound that made him know that he had new things to learn about fear. It was a distant sound, faint and wavering, but he knew it. It was the baying of a pack of hounds.

Rainsford knew he could do one of two things. He could stay where he was and wait. That was suicide. He could flee. That was postponing the inevitable. For a moment he stood there, thinking. An idea that held a wild chance came to him, and, tightening his belt, he headed away from the swamp. The baying of the hounds drew nearer, then still nearer, nearer, ever nearer. On a ridge Rainsford climbed a tree. Down a watercourse, not a quarter of a mile away, he could see the bush moving. Straining his eyes, he saw the lean figure of General Zaroff; just ahead of him Rainsford made out another figure whose wide shoulders surged through the tall jungle weeds; it was the giant Ivan, and he seemed pulled forward by some unseen force; Rainsford knew that Ivan must be holding the pack in leash.

They would be on him any minute now. His mind worked frantically. He thought of a native trick he had learned in Uganda. He slid down the tree. He caught hold of a springy young sapling and to it he fastened his hunting knife, with the blade pointing down the trail; with a bit of wild grapevine he tied back the sapling. Then he ran for his life. The hounds raised their voices as they hit the fresh scent. Rainsford knew now how an animal at bay feels.

He had to stop to get his breath. The baying of the hounds stopped abruptly, and Rainsford's heart stopped too. They must have reached the knife.

He shinned excitedly up a tree and looked back. His pursuers had stopped. But the hope that was in Rainsford's brain when he climbed died, for he saw in the shallow valley that General Zaroff was still on his feet. But Ivan was not. The knife, driven by the recoil of the springing tree, had not wholly failed.

Rainsford had hardly tumbled to the ground when the pack took up the cry again.

'Nerve, nerve, nerve!' he panted, as he dashed along. A blue gap showed between the trees dead ahead. Ever nearer drew the hounds. Rainsford forced himself on toward that gap. He reached it. It was the shore of the sea. Across a cove he could see the gloomy grey stone of the château. Twenty feet below him the sea rumbled and hissed. Rainsford hesitated. He heard the hounds. Then he leaped far out into the sea . . .

When the general and his pack reached the place by the sea, the Cossack stopped. For some minutes he stood regarding the blue-green expanse of water. He shrugged his shoulders. Then he sat down, took a drink of brandy from a silver flask, lit a perfumed cigarette, and hummed a bit from 'Madame Butterfly.'

General Zaroff had an exceedingly good dinner in his great panelled dining hall that evening. With it he had a bottle of Pol Roger and half a bottle of Chambertin. Two slight annoyances kept him from perfect enjoyment. One was the thought that it would be difficult to replace Ivan; the other was that his quarry had escaped him; of course the American hadn't played the game — so thought the general as he tasted his after-dinner liqueur. In his library he read, to soothe himself, from the works of Marcus Aurelius. At ten he went up to his bedroom. He was deliciously tired, he said to himself, as he locked himself in. There was a little moonlight, so, before turning on his light, he went to the window and looked down at the courtyard. He could see the great hounds, and he called: 'Better luck another time,' to them. Then he switched on the light.

A man, who had been hiding in the curtains of the bed, was standing there.

'Rainsford!' screamed the general. 'How in God's name did you get here?'

'Swam,' said Rainsford. 'I found it quicker than walking through the jungle.'

The general sucked in his breath and smiled. 'I congratulate you,' he said. 'You have won the game.'

Rainsford did not smile. 'I am still a beast at bay,' he said, in a low, hoarse voice. 'Get ready, General Zaroff.'

The general made one of his deepest bows. 'I see,' he said.

'Splendid! One of us is to furnish a repast for the hounds. The other will sleep in this very excellent bed. On guard, Rainsford.' ...

He had never slept in a better bed, Rainsford decided.

Follow On

The aim of all the activities in this section is to add to your enjoyment and understanding of the stories in this anthology. Some stories you may simply want to read and remember, others you may want to talk and write about, others may spark-off memories and further ideas.

The suggestions for activities can be used to help you build up a folder for the coursework element of the General Certificate of Secondary Education. These fall into three broad areas:

Before reading — enabling you to anticipate and speculate about what is going to happen.

During reading — building up a picture of what is going on and what may happen next.

After reading — allowing time to reflect on the setting, events, characters, issues and themes within the stories; giving opportunities for discussion, and for personal, critical and discursive writing.

Many of the activities will involve a mixture of individual, group and whole class work. You may not want to attempt all of the suggested activities but choose ones which particularly interest you. In some cases you may wish to ignore them altogether and devise an activity or response of your own.

General Activities

Before reading

▶ Read an extract, poem, play or short story which:
   — takes up similar themes or issues
   — presents characters/settings in similar/contrasting ways
   — is written in a similar/contrasting style or genre.

▶ Take some general issues or questions raised in the story and discuss them in advance to find out how much you and others know and what opinions you have about them. After reading the story, discuss how far your ideas and opinions may have changed.

▶ Use the titles and/or the first few paragraphs to speculate and predict what the story may be about.

▶ Take some quotations from the story and speculate how the story will develop.

During reading

▶ Stop at various points during reading, and review what has happened so far, then predict what might happen next or how the story may develop.

▶ Stop at various points and discuss why writers have made certain decisions and what alternatives were open to them.

▶ Decide who is telling or speaking the story.

▶ Look out for important quotations that help reveal the meaning of the story.

▶ Make notes and observations on plot, character, relationships between characters, style and the way the narrative works.

▶ Consider the various issues, themes or questions relating to the story which you discussed before reading.

▶ Build up a visual picture of the setting in order to work out its significance in the story or to represent it as a diagram.

▶ Discuss a number of statements about the story and decide which best conveys what the story is about.

▶ Prepare a dramatic reading of parts of the text.

▶ Use the story as a stimulus for personal and imaginative writing:
— writing stories/plays/poems on a similar theme
— writing stories/plays/poems in a similar style, genre or with a similar structure.

▶ Discuss and write imaginative reconstructions or extensions of the text:
— rewriting the story from another character's point of view
— writing a scene which occurs before the story begins
— continuing beyond the end of the story
— writing an alternative ending
— changing the narrative from the first to the third-person and vice versa
— experimenting with style and form
— picking a point in the story where the action takes a turn in direction and rewriting the rest of the story in a different way.

▶ Represent some of the ideas, issues and themes in the story for a particular purpose and audience:
— enacting a public inquiry or tribunal
— conducting an interview for TV or radio
— writing a newspaper report or press release
— writing a letter to a specified person or organisation
— giving an eye-witness report.

▶ Select passages from the story for film or radio scripting; act out the rehearsed script for a live audience, audio or video taping.

▶ Write critically or discursively about the story, or comparing one or more story, focusing on:
— the meaning of the title
— character, plot and structure
— style, tone, use of dialect, language
— build up of tension, use of climax, humour, pathos, etc.
— endings
— themes and issues.

No Witchcraft for Sale

Before reading

▶ This story is set in Zimbabwe. When Doris Lessing wrote the story, Zimbabwe was still a British colony, known as Southern Rhodesia. At that time, the small white minority held all the political and economic power. The majority black population had no say in the running of their country.

Find out what you can about the government of Zimbabwe today. Discuss the contrasts between this and the system of *apartheid*, which operates in South Africa.

▶ Read the first two paragraphs down to:
'Mrs Farquar was fond of the old cook because of his love for her child' (page 7).
How might this story develop?

During reading

▶ As you read the story pay particular attention to the contrast in life styles of the blacks and the whites.

After reading

▶ Discuss why you think Doris Lessing wrote this story.

▶ What kind of people are the Farquars?
Compare their treatment of their black servants with the Aubignys in 'Désirée's Baby'.

▶ What words would you use to describe this story — sad, moving, provocative, humane, realistic, compassionate, warm, sensitive, vivid, disturbing? Make a list in groups.

▶ Working with a partner discuss what you understand by the following phrases:
— 'distorted by great purple oozing protuberances' (page 9)
— 'the darker tracts of the human mind — which is the black man's heritage' (page 10)
— 'come salting the tail of a fabulous bush-secret' (page 11)

▶ Discuss Gideon's reaction when he is asked to reveal the whereabouts of the miraculous root.

▶ 'The Farquars and the scientist had different motives for wanting to see the new drug produced'. Do you agree with this statement? Give reasons.

▶ 'These things get exaggerated in the telling'.
Write a story — sad or amusing — in which the central character lets his or her imagination run riot.

▶ When the scientist arrives back at the laboratory in town, he relates his visit to the Farquar's homestead to a colleague. Write out their conversation.

▶ Can you remember an occasion when you, or someone close to you, had an accident which required medical treatment? Describe what happened and try to recall your thoughts and feelings at the time.

▶ Write the letter Mrs Farquar sends to her sister in England in which she gives an account of Teddy's ordeal.

▶ Discuss the reasons why the author may have chosen 'No Witch-craft for Sale' as her title. Write up the conclusions you arrive at.

▶ To find relief from the suffering of prolonged illness some people have turned from what is called 'orthodox medicine' to acupuncture, herbal remedies or faith healing. What are your views on such alternative medicine?

▶ Write a story in which superstition plays an important part.

The Rose Garden

| Before reading |

▶ What does the title suggest this story might be about?

▶ In 'The Rose Garden' Mike Haywood describes one form of environmental pollution. Before reading the story find out what everyone in the group knows and thinks about this issue.

| During reading |

▶ In this story the author makes considerable use of the five senses in describing the scene. While you are reading the story note down any references to taste and smell.

▶ Stop reading at the *end* of the paragraph beginning: 'After five. And it's raining. Buses go by full of people' (page 16).
How would you describe the mood created by the author?

| After reading |

▶ In pairs discuss why you think the author decided to write this story. Was he trying to say something in particular?

▶ In groups discuss what Alan Plater says about Mike Haywood's writing:
'His work had its roots in urban speech — you can hear the echoes of shop floor, bowling green and back yard walls — and he transformed this material into a poetry that spoke for the people with a rare tang.'
Can you think of any other characteristic ingredient of Mike Hayward's writing?

▶ As he travels home the following evening Charlie recalls winning the top prize from the School of Art and Craft back in 1949. Recount his memories.

▶ Write a short play based on a conversation you have heard or taken part in on a bus or train.

▶ 'When tha leaves school tha mon come wi' me to mill,' says Charlie's father.
Write a script in which a young person, against his or her parents' wishes, decides on a particular career.

▶ What sort of person is Charlie Brown? Write about one day in his life.

▶ 'The Rose Garden' is set in industrial South Yorkshire. Compare the local dialect used by the author with that used in the area where you live.

▶ What effect does the writer want to create by ending the story in the way he does? How did you expect the story to end? Discuss in small groups alternative endings and how the story might be continued.

▶ 'Charlie was a moving man.' Write a short story about someone who makes his or her living travelling the country.

▶ 'I like something waiting good and hot, something decent. I'm not one for catch penny suppers — not me,' says the little chap on the bus. Later Charlie sees him in the chip shop. Why did the little chap lie and why do you think he was weeping?

▶ Here is a poem written by a fifth year student:

> Nothing to see but back-to-backs
> Of crumbling brick and peeling paint,
> And dirty pubs of dingy brown,
> And empty shops with windows cracked.
>
> Nothing to hear but the chuddering van,
> Screeching cars and the grumbling bus
> And crumpled papers and plastic cups,
> Crunched in the gutter with rattling cans.
>
> Nothing to smell but the greasy stench
> Of chip-shop fat from the dirty caff,
> The stink of sweat and the toilet waft
> From the vagrant propped on the Town Hall bench.
>
> Nothing to feel but the emptiness,
> Nothing to feel,
> Nothing.
>
> *Geraldine Morton*

Write a poem or description of an inner city.
Write a contrasting description of a rural area.

The Pond

Before reading

▶ Read the first few paragraphs down to:
    'He froze.' (page 19)
    What do you imagine this story is about?

During reading

▶ Stop at the following points in the story and predict what you think will happen next:
    'He saw the frog listen.' (page 19)
    'Suddenly he lowered his needle. He listened.' (page 23)
    'He knew there was no one to hear him.' (page 24)

▶ As you read the story select any sentences or phrases which strike you as particularly unusual or effective. Explain their meanings in the context of the story and say how they add to the overall atmosphere.

| *After reading* |

▶ The dissection of animals is sometimes considered essential in developing biological skill and understanding.and in some school biology courses it plays an important role.

    Organise a debate on the topic: 'To cut or not to cut' in which the arguments for and against dissection are discussed.

    You may find the following points, taken from an R.S.P.C.A. leaflet, helpful:

FOR	AGAINST
1 To gain knowledge and understanding of the internal structures of different species.	1 It involves the taking of life.
2 To gain personal experience of both the fragility and strength of fresh tissues.	2 The rearing and killing of animals for dissection may involve suffering.
3 Improvement of learning through active involvement and first hand experience.	3 It may cheapen the value of animal life for pupils and encourage cruelty to animals.
4 As a preparation for such careers as that of doctor or veterinary surgeon.	4 Because some pupils may find dissection upsetting and distasteful, they may be discouraged from studying biology.

▶ Write a conversation between the village postman and a neighbour in which they discuss their impressions of the old man.

▶ Write the report which appears in the local newspaper following the discovery of the body. Give it an eye-catching headline.

▶ In small groups, discuss your reactions to this story. Did you find it silly, disturbing, confusing, entertaining, sickening, amazing?

▶ A week later an official inquiry into the old man's death takes place. It is chaired by the County Coroner and the following witnesses are called to give evidence:
— a neighbour of the old man's
— the policeman who discovered the body
— the police pathologist who carried out the post-mortem
  Write the transcript of the proceedings or act out the inquest.

▶ The story reaches a gruesome and unexpected climax. Discuss the ending.

The Goat and the Stars

Before reading

▶ What does the title suggest this story is about?
  Think carefully about the different meanings it could have.

During reading

▶ Stop at the following points during reading and predict what you think might happen next:
— 'THIS MEANS YOU!' (at the end of paragraph 2, page 27)
— '. . . the kid at his side, on the string, like a little dog.' (page 28).

After reading

▶ What difference would it have made to the story as a whole if it had ended two paragraphs before, with the words:
  'It was clear that the notice did not mean him at all'? (page 30)
  What other endings are possible?

▶ Write an essay on the title: 'The Misunderstanding'.

▶ In *The Modern Short Story*, H. E. Bates writes:
> 'The structure of the short story is too delicate, too tenuous for a load of verbal pomposity . . . Atmosphere and precision, however subtly concealed, are in fact two of the cardinal points in the art of the short story writer.'

Do these comments help you to appreciate rather more 'The Goat and the Stars'?

▶ Compare the storytelling technique of H. E. Bates with that of O. Henry and Roald Dahl. You might consider:
— structure
— handling of ideas and action
— characters
— use of dialogue
— description
— significant detail
— mood and atmosphere
— opening and closing paragraphs.

▶ 'The Goat and the Stars', in many ways, is a sad story but there are flashes of humour, such as the incident in the church. Do these amusing touches detract from the overall mood of the short story?

▶ Write the conversation which might have taken place between the Vicar and the Usher about the little boy who brought a goat to church.

▶ Write the account the boy might give to his parents when he arrives home that evening.

▶ Write a poem or an account about a particularly disappointing Christmas.

Désirée's Baby

| Before reading |

▶ What does the title of this story suggest it may be about?

▶ Read the first three paragraphs and discuss where and when the story is set.

During reading

► Make notes on Désirée's changing feelings as the story develops.

► In this story the author uses a number of similes (that is, when she says one thing is *like* another). Make a note of the similes you come across and comment on their effectiveness.

► Stop reading at the *end* of the paragraph beginning:
   'When the letter reached Désirée . . .' (page 35)
   Predict how the story will end.

After reading

► The setting for 'Désirée's Baby' is Louisiana in America's 'Deep South', when the white landowners used black slave labour. What do you learn from this story about the relationship between master and slave and the attitudes of the whites to their black servants?

► Write three entries in Désirée's journal:
   — on the day the story opens
   — on the day she writes to her mother
   — on the day she receives her mother's reply.

► Write the conversation between Zandrine and Négrillon on the day of Désirée's death.

► Désirée's past was a mystery. Write about the events leading up to her discovery at Valmondé.

► Write the letter Madame Valmondé sends to Armand telling him of Désirée's death.
   Write Armand's reply in which he may or may not reveal the contents of his mother's letter.

► The story ends on a tragic and despairing note.
   Working in pairs, consider the following questions:
   What difference would it have made to the story as a whole if it had ended five paragraphs before with the words 'and she did not come back again'? (page 36).
   Why did the author decide to end the story in the way she did?

► Write an imaginative account based on the title:
   'A Secret from the Past'.

► Do you think the ending indicates that Armand knew he was 'cursed' before Désirée left?

How do you think the story might have differed if he had revealed the contents of the letter.

In discussing this consider how different people might react:
— Désirée
— his slaves
— other white landowners.

The Landlady

| Before reading |

▶ Read the first five paragraphs down to: 'They were amazing' (page 38). What sort of person is Billy Weaver?

| During reading |

▶ The longer Billy spends in the old lady's house the more uneasy and perplexed he becomes about certain things. As you read the story make a note of any strange features of the house and examples of the landlady's odd behaviour.

| After reading |

▶ Write the newspaper report of the disappearance of Christopher Mulholland and Gregory Temple.

▶ Imagine you are leaving home, relatives and friends to live and work in another part of the country. Write several entries in your diary recording your first impressions of the new people you meet.

▶ Two youths break into the landlady's house. Describe what they discover and the outcome of the burglary. Try to capture the atmosphere of the sinister house, the smells which linger and the staring eyes of the preserved animals.

▶ Imagine that Billy's father traces him to the old lady's house. Write a short play about his conversation with the landlady.

▶ In the poem and the description which follow a landlord and a landlady are described, both as unpleasant as the old lady in the story. Using the ideas in both these pieces, in Dahl's story and any ideas of your own, write an account in which you consider the characteristics of both a good and a bad landlord or landlady.

Ballad of the landlord

Landlord, landlord,
My roof has sprung a leak
Don't you 'member I told you about it
Way last week?

Landlord, landlord,
These steps is broken down.
When you come up yourself
It's a wonder you don't fall down.

Ten Bucks you say I owe you?
Ten Bucks you say is due?
Well, that's Ten Bucks more'n I'll pay you
Till you fix this house up new.

What? You gonna get eviction orders?
You gonna cut off my heat?
You gonna take my furniture and
Throw it in the street?

Um-huh! You talking high and mighty.
Talk on — till you get through.
You ain't gonna be able to say a word
If I land my fist on you.

Police! Police!
Come and get this man!
He's trying to ruin the government
And overturn the land!

Copper's whistle!
Patrol bell!
Arrest.
Precinct Station.
Iron cell.
Headlines in press:

MAN THREATENS LANDLORD

TENANT HELD NO BAIL

JUDGE GIVES NEGRO 90 DAYS IN COUNTY JAIL

Langston Hughes

The Landlady

Mrs Hardy resembled one of those huge stone statues you find on Easter Island. As she stood motionless on the scrubbed steps of the Happy Haven Holiday Hotel with her fixed stony expression and her muscular arms folded across her mountainous bosom, she put the fear of God into her paying guests.

As children we went every year to the Happy Haven, Skegness. I do not know why because after every holiday my father vowed never again to enter that forbidding doorway. But back again we went.

Mrs Hardy was a large woman — and I mean large — with hooded eyes like a hawk's and an expression any self respecting basilisk would have been proud of. My brother Alex used to run up and down the sands kicking his feet in the air and giving the Nazi salute while shrieking a 'Heil Hardy!' But back in the boarding house under her stony stare he was like a mouse.

The hallway had a bowl of dusty plastic roses above which was a poster with 'Rules of the House' writ large: Don't do this, must do that, can't go here! When my father burnt a hole in the bedroom carpet we all had a sleepless night and once when we were less than ecstatic about her toad-in-the-hole she barred the door with her formidable bulk until our plates were empty.

Mary Sullivan

▶ Imagine you are adapting this story for television. Write a script. You might wish to use the following notes as a guide:
— Use only the right hand side of the paper leaving space for the producer to make notes.
— Speakers' names, directions and descriptions are all written in capitals. Only the actual words spoken are written in lower case.
— Do not include too much dialogue. Television, unlike radio, is visual and facial expressions can often make dialogue unnecessary.
— Scenes should be kept to a minimum.
— Make an outline plan of the different scenes.
— Write clear directions for actors/actresses and the camera crew. Act out the play with your group.

▶ In groups discuss whether you agree or disagree with the following statements:
  — Roald Dahl leaves too much to the reader's imagination.
  — the best feature of this story is the strong element of suspense.
  — Billy Weaver was particularly naïve not to have realised much earlier what the old lady was up to.

▶ Imagine you are the landlady's next paying guest. Relate your experiences.

Vendetta

Before reading

▶   'An eye for an eye and
       a tooth for a tooth'
       What are your views on revenge?

During reading

▶ Read the introductory paragraph (page 47) where the author, using carefully chosen details, conveys a vivid picture of Bonifacio. Note down any phrasing which you find particularly effective. Does this paragraph give you any clues about what might happen later in the story?

After reading

▶ Below are a list of statements about the story. Working in pairs choose those with which you agree and explain why:
  — the old woman was justified in taking the law into her own hands.
  — when she found out where her son's murderer had taken refuge, the old woman should have informed the police and left it to them.
  — if she had been found out, the old woman should have been tried for murder.
  — the Widow Saverini was a cold, calculating and unfeeling old woman who having murdered Ravolati slept well that night.
  — the Widow Saverini was a heartbroken, maternal and courageous old woman who believed she had done no wrong.

— if the Widow Saverini had killed Ravolati immediately, it would have been easier to forgive. It was the planning and cold-bloodedness which made her crime that much worse.

▶ Write two short newspaper articles — one reporting the 'treacherous stabbing' of Antoine Saverini, the other giving an account of Nicolas Ravolati's murder. Give each an eye-catching headline.

▶ Write a statement given to the police by a neighbour of Ravolati describing the 'old beggar man' and his 'lean black dog'.

▶ Discuss what aspects of Italian life are illustrated in this story.

▶ Before she dies the Widow Saverini decides to relate what happened. Write her confession which includes her reason for taking Nicolas Ravolati's life.

▶ Write a brief outline of the plot of the story, a synopsis of not more than 150 words.

▶ Write an account of a play or film you have seen or a story you have read, in which revenge is the main theme.

▶ Thinking about the story as a whole, discuss in groups what makes 'Vendetta' such a powerful and compelling piece of writing?

▶ Using first person narrative ('I') imagine you are the Widow Saverini and tell your story of the Vendetta.

▶ Using the following quotation from 'Vendetta' — 'You shall be avenged!' — write your own story.

The Birthday Present

Before reading

▶ This is a ghost story! In groups share with each other any stories about strange or supernatural happenings which you have experienced or heard about.

During reading

▶ Stop at the following points in the reading and predict what you think may happen next:
'But it didn't happen like that.' (page 58)
'I had one goal — HOME!' (page 58).

▶ What are your first impressions of Fatty Scrimshaw?

▶ Discuss the advantages and disadvantages of living in a tower block of flats.

▶ Talk to your grandparents or an older person who remembers anything about the last War. Make a tape recording or take notes about any interesting accounts and anecdotes. Use this as the starting point for a story of your own.

▶ Improvise the scene which takes place later in the pub when the football fans relate the strange events which occurred on their way home from the match.

▶ If you were given the opportunity of interviewing Marjorie Darke, what questions would you ask her about this story, or about what she says in her personal essay?

▶ 'The Birthday Present' is very different from other stories in the collection. For example, the author uses first person narrative which gives a more personal and intimate flavour to the story and great use is made of colloquial, chatty language. Discuss these differences and any others you can find. (Note what Marjorie Darke says about the writer's 'voice' in her essay.)

▶ 'After all', says Kevin at the end of the story, 'how am I to know when I might need saving again?'
    Write a further episode when Stan comes to the rescue.

The Ransom of Red Chief

▶ What does the title of this story suggest it may be about?

▶ Read the first three paragraphs and discuss:
    — the setting for the story
    — what you learn about the narrator
    — the style in which the story is written
    — how you think the story will develop.

▶ One of the characters in 'The Ransom of Red Chief' enjoys using long and unusual words. As you read the story pick out those words and phrases and suggest what he *actually* means!

▶ Make a note of the various antics of Red Chief. Which do you think is the funniest; the cruellest; the most outrageous?

After reading

▶ In what ways are Sam and Bill untypical kidnappers?

▶ In pairs discuss the reactions of:
  — Red Chief to his kidnapping
  — the inhabitants of Summit on hearing that the boy is 'lost or stolen'
  — Ebenezer Dorset on receiving the ransom note
  — the kidnappers on receiving Ebenezer Dorset's reply.

▶ Write an amusing account about a spoilt and mischievous child like Red Chief.

▶ Write a short newspaper feature covering the disappearance of the boy.

▶ Write a conversation between the postmaster and a customer in which they discuss the boy's disappearance.

▶ Many years later Red Chief recalls his adventures with Sam and Bill and tells his own small boy the story of his kidnapping. Write about his reminiscence.

▶ Continue the story in the same style as O. Henry and write about what happens to Red Chief on his return home.

▶ On his return home Red Chief is interviewed by the Sheriff. Write the script.

Salt on a Snake's Tail

Before reading

▶ This story explores the disturbing subject of racial prejudice. Before reading discuss the following questions:

— What are your views on racism?
— What parts can schools play in developing good race relations?
— What steps should be taken to stop racist attacks?

| During reading |

▶ Make notes on the main features of Asian life in Britain which are described in this story.

▶ Stop reading at the following parts in the story and try to predict what will happen next:
— 'Bengalis love to talk big talk,' his father said (page 78)
— 'Jolil didn't reply' (page 84)
— 'There was a flash of spite in his face' (page 87).

| After reading |

▶ What do you understand by the proverb: 'Put salt on a snake's tail'?
Find out about proverbs from other countries.

▶ Improvise the conversation in which Mr Miah and Kazi-sahab discuss how life in Britain has affected the young Asians.

▶ In this story Mr Miah is a hypocrite; he preaches pacifism and obedience to the Koran and yet ultimately resorts to violence.
What are your views on Mr Miah's action?

▶ 'The best brought up children are those who have seen their parents as they are. Hypocrisy is not the parent's first duty.'
(George Bernard Shaw: *Man and Superman*)
Do you agree with this comment? Is there a case for parents being hypocritical?

▶ Write the newspaper article reporting the stabbing of the white boy.

▶ Jolil escapes the grim reality of his life by dreaming of Bruce Lee and the secrets of Kung Fu. Write a short play in which the main character escapes into a world of fantasy.

▶ Discuss the feeling and problems someone might experience when moving from one country to live in another.

▶ Jolil is embarrassed and shamed by his father's actions. Is he justified in feeling as he does?

▶ The responsibilities of a parent might include:
 — to provide shelter, clothes and food
 — to give love and affection
 — to protect and care for
 — to encourage and support
 — to exercise discipline.
  Are there any further 'duties' you would add to the list?
  To what extent does Mr Miah fulfil these responsibilities?

▶ Devise a 'mock trial' in which Mr Miah appears, accused of 'actual bodily harm'.
  You might wish to use the following sequence of the case:
 — Mr Miah is charged by the *Clerk of the Court* and pleads either guilty or not guilty
 — the *Prosecution* outlines the facts of the case
 — the *Prosecution* calls its witnesses: friends of the wounded boy; investigating police officer; anyone who saw the attack; the boy who was stabbed
 — the *Defence counsel* cross-examines the witnesses on the evidence they have just given
 — the *Defence* opens its case and calls the defence witnesses: Jolil; Khalil; Mr Miah (the defendant)
 — the *Prosecution* cross-examines these witnesses
 — the *Defence* sums up its case and urges the jury to return a verdict of 'not guilty'
 — the *Prosecution* concludes its case and asks for a 'guilty' verdict
 — the *Judge* sums up the trial, reviewing the evidence and pointing out any inconsistencies or unexplained details
 — the *Jury* retires and, under the direction of the *foreman* or *forewoman*, considers its verdict
 — the *Jury* returns, the verdict is pronounced and the *Judge* delivers sentence.
  (Mr Miah would plead self-defence but the Prosecution would argue it was an unprovoked attack.)

▶ The poem 'Immigrants' takes up the issues of injustice, discrimination and prejudice which are explored in several of the stories included in this anthology.
  Compare how the different writers attempt to make their point and affect their readers.

Immigrants

The chief change
I've noted
among
White Folks is
now they talkin
bout us in code.
Like,
Stateside when they
say:
crime in the streets or
welfare cheats
they talkin bout us.
An in Britain
when they say
Immigrants, guess
who they mean?
I mean, they got
Cypriots, Pakistanis,
Indians, Spanish an
Italians,
but, even if yo
Great-great-great-great
Grandaddy was the
Dude turned on Ol Will
in a stable an
caused him to write

Othello, you still
an Immigrant if yo
skin is other than
fish-belly white.
Quite!
Maybe it takes as
long to become
A Black Briton
as it does to grow
them Midlands lawns
nobody but birds
walk on.
That would be cool
if they laid the
same standards on
everybody else come
here since the
Norman Invasion.
Like,
how bout that
German Lady layin
up in Buckingham Palace?
I mean,
how come the Queen
ain't un
Immu-grunt?

Sam Greenlee

The Vacancy

Before reading

▶ Read the first few paragraphs of the story down to:
  '. . . you could never tell if they were on automatic' (page 94)
  Are there any clues in the story which help you predict what this
  story may be about?

▶ Discuss in pairs what you imagine life will be like in.the year 2020.

| During reading |

▶ Make a list of things referred to in the story which are different from those in present day society.

| After reading |

▶ What are your first impressions of: Miss Feather; Mr Boston?

▶ Describe the experiences of another applicant keen to fill the vacancy.

▶ Suggest some alternative titles for this story giving reasons why you think they are appropriate.

▶ What are the ingredients of a good science fiction story?
   Write a fantasy set in the year 2020.

▶ Adapt 'The Vacancy' for radio. The following notes may be used as a guide:
   — give yourself a wide margin for the speakers' names and any rough production notes
   — underline everything which is not spoken
   — write speakers' names in capital letters
   — sound effects are indicated by FX. They can be used for the setting of the drama
   — begin and end scenes with fading. Music could be used to begin and end your adaptation
   — write directions for the actors: use of pause; tone of voice; expressions.

▶ What are your views on the ending of the story?

The Most Dangerous Game

| Before reading |

▶ What does the title suggest this story might be about?

▶ A character in this story says that hunting is 'the best sport in the world'. What is the attraction of hunting for some people?
   Find out what others in the group feel about fox hunting and hare coursing.

| During reading |

▶ While reading the story pay particular attention to the way the author builds up the tension.

▶ Note down any features of style and structure which you think are effective and which hold your attention: features such as vivid description, use of unusual words and phrases, interesting comparisons, memories, significant details.

| After reading |

▶ What part of this story remains particularly in your mind?

▶ Write the entry in Captain Nielsen's log for the day of Rainsford's disappearance.

▶ Below are some statements made by General Zaroff. Working with a partner discuss them:
  — 'God makes some men poets. Some He makes kings, some beggars. Me He made a hunter' (page 113)
  — 'The animal had nothing but his legs and his instinct. Instinct is no match for reason' (page 114)
  — 'Life is for the strong, to be lived by the strong, and, if needs be, taken by the strong' (page 115).

▶ Write the item which is read in the television news telling of Rainsford's disappearance in the Caribbean. You might include a small biography of this world famous big game hunter.

▶ 'The Most Dangerous Game' was made into an early black and white horror movie. The director decided to change some aspects of the story; for example it was re-titled 'The Hounds of Zaroff' and a heroine was introduced.

  Imagine you are given the task of adapting this story for the screen, what changes to the original story would you make?

  Pick out a scene from 'The Most Dangerous Game' and dramatise it. The following ideas may be useful:
  — read the scene several times
  — edit where necessary
  — leave space for production notes
  — speech marks are unnecessary
  — include details of speakers' reactions, expressions, tones of voice, feelings and movements
  — include details of camera shots (close-ups, distance shots), sound effects, flashbacks and music.

▶ Write a horror story of your own which contains all the typical ingredients. You might use the following ideas:

Geographical Setting: a land of mists, fogs, torrential rains and whistling winds; of stunted shrubs and gnarled trees; of screeching owls and howling wolves

Buildings: grey-stoned, turreted, crumbling castles with leaded windows; iron-studded doors and long dark corridors; châteaux with dark dungeons; mouldy hangings, rusting armour and flickering candles

Characters: elegant, Eastern European aristocrat from an ancient family; old retainer with ashen hair and sallow complexion; mute servant of incredible strength; the unsuspecting hero/heroine

Structure: setting the scene, building up the atmosphere, filling out descriptions and incidents with details designed to scare the reader who should be made to feel the impending horror from the moment the story begins. The final agony should be continually anticipated and only reached after the reader has been really frightened.

Titles:
  Castle D'Eath
  Vendetta of Blood
  Count Alucard
  The Return of General Zaroff
  Island of Doom

▶ After his ordeal Rainsford returns to America where he gives a television interview in which he relates the story of 'The Most Dangerous Game'.
  Write the script.

▶ Discuss what the effect would have been on this story had the last line been omitted. Devise some alternative last lines.

▶ 'On guard!' (page 126)
  Describe the fight to the death between Rainsford and the General.

▶ Continue the story and describe what happened the next morning.

Further ideas for group and individual work

▶ Why do you think the editor of this collection chose *Sweet and Sour* for the title? Can you think of an equally appropriate title?

▶ Discuss the cover illustration. Design an alternative.

▶ If you were asked to illustrate this collection with line drawings and photographs which incidents would you depict? Give reasons for your choice.

▶ Many authors base their writing on actual incidents which have occurred in their lives. Which of these stories do you think were based on real events and experiences?

▶ The stories in this collection explore a wide variety of themes:
  family relationships   the generation gap
  prejudice   childhood
  disappointment   loneliness
  injustice   people's treatment of animals
  revenge   different cultures
  genre: science fiction, mystery and suspense.
  Discuss these and any other thematic links you have discovered. Compare and contrast how the different writers explore some of the themes.

▶ Which of the stories has the most:
  compelling opening   surprising ending
  readable plot   interesting character?
  Compare your views with others in the group.

▶ Compare several of the short stories in the collection in terms of: title; setting; structure; characters; use of language; style of writing.

▶ Write a review of your favourite short story in the collection.
  Write a further review of the story you enjoyed the least.

▶ Discuss in small groups which of the short stories is:
  the saddest   the most compassionate
  the least interesting   the most enjoyable
  the most realistic   the most amusing
  the most thought-provoking.

▶ In her essay on page 61 Marjorie Darke says that 'setting the atmosphere in just the right way can make or break any story'.

Choose a story which you've particularly enjoyed and say how you feel the author's setting of atmosphere 'makes' the story.

▶ Which of the short stories would make a good film or television play? Give reasons.

▶ What motivates the characters in the various stories? What makes them act in the way they do?

Choose one of the stories in the collection and, working in small groups, take it in turns to play some of the characters who appear. They might be interviewed by the others in the group and asked to explain why they behaved as they did.

▶ Which of the characters in the short stories did you most:
    identify with   envy
    dislike   feel sympathy for?
    Write your own stories which feature these four characters.

▶ Compare how three different authors (a) introduce their stories; (b) bring their stories to a climax?

▶ Using a cassette recorder (a) present a dramatic reading of one of the stories, complete with sound effects and music; (b) record your general impressions of two stories.

▶ In the 'Preface' to *Four Countries*, William Plomer writes: 'A short story must lead us into the secrets of other people's lives.' Which of the stories in this collection do you feel best achieves this?

▶ Devise a quiz or a board game based on one of these stories.

▶ Which of the short stories stays particularly in your memory?
    Can you say why?

▶ Have any of the stories in this collection made you re-think your opinions or helped you better to understand aspects of the world in which you live?

▶ In two of the short stories in the collection the authors use the first person 'I', while in the remainder a third person narrator is used. What are the advantages and disadvantages of the different types of narration? Rewrite one of the stories changing the narrative point of view.

▶ Compare two amusing stories and try to analyse how the author creates the comedy.

Further Reading

No Witchcraft for Sale

Doris Lessing was born in 1919 and moved at an early age to Rhodesia (now Zimbabwe) where her father managed a large farm. Much of her writing is about her life in South Africa and Rhodesia where she lived for twenty-five years. She came to live in England in 1949. She writes sensitively and convincingly about ordinary people, but beneath the apparently simple plots are contained important truths about how we live and relate to one another. 'No Witchcraft for Sale' is from the collection *This was the Old Chief's Country*, (Panther).

Related reading:

Unwinding Threads: Writing by Women in Africa, selected and edited by Charlotte H. Bruner, Heinemann African Writers Series (1985)

Mouth Open, Story Jump Out, Grace Hallworth, Methuen (1984)

Poems, edited by Michael Harrison and Christopher Stuart-Clark, Oxford University Press (1979)

Jet, a Gift to all the Family, Geoffrey Kilner, Puffin (1976)

A Walk in the Night, Alex La Guma, Heinemann African Writers Series (1968)

To Kill a Mockingbird, Harper Lee, Pan (1974)

The Grass is Singing and *The Habit of Loving*, Doris Lessing, Panther (1980 and 1973)

Bandiet: Seven Years in a South African Prison, Hugh Lewin, Heinemann African Writers Series (1982)

Journey to Jo'Burg, a South African Story, Beverley Naidoo, Longman Knockouts (1985)

The Rose Garden

Mike Haywood was born near Rotherham in 1934. Leaving school at fifteen, he became a painter's apprentice before joining the Royal Marines. Later he worked as a labourer in the steel mills. He began attending evening classes where his creative talent was soon recognised by his teacher, who suggested he apply to Ruskin College, Oxford.

'The Rose Garden' is taken from *Mike Haywood—some poems, plays, stories and sketches* (Rotherham M.B.C.), a varied collection of Mike Haywood's work published two years after his death in 1973. It contains the characteristic ingredients of his writing: humour, warmth, the vigorous speech of working class Northerners, a clear and lively language and astute social observation.

Related reading:

The Human Element and other stories, Stan Barstow, Longman Imprint (1970)

One Way Only, Gwen Grant, Heinemann (1983)

Love on the Dole, Walter Greenwood, Cape (1966)

Northern Childhood: The Balaclava Story, George Layton, Longman Knockouts (1976)

Northern Childhood: The Fib and other stories, George Layton, Longman Knockouts (1978)

Late Night on Watling Street, Bill Naughton, Longman Imprint (1979)

A Ragged Schooling, Robert Roberts, Fontana/Collins (1976)

This Sporting Life, David Storey, Longman Heritage of Literature Series (1974)

The Loneliness of the Long Distance Runner, Longman Heritage of Literature Series (1966)

There is a Happy Land, Keith Waterhouse, Longman Imprint (1968)

The Pond

Nigel Kneale's great skill as a writer of frightening and macabre stories is well illustrated in his collection *Tomato Cain and Other Stories* from which 'The Pond' is taken. In addition to writing tales of terror he also produced the *Quatermass* serials and the terrifying and sinister supernatural film *The Stone Tape*.

Related reading:

The Gruesome Book, Ramsey Campbell, Piccolo (1983)
House of Fear, Jan Carew, Longman Knockouts (1981)
Ghosts That Haunt You, compiled by Aidan Chambers, Kestrel (1980)
Thrillers, Chillers and Killers, Helen Hoke, Dent (1979)
Ghostly and Ghastly, Barbara Ireson, Hamlyn (1977)
Nothing to be Afraid of, Jan Mark, Puffin (1980)
Ed. McBain's Mystery Book, Kirby McCauley Ltd (1961)
Ghost of the Glen, Alan McLean, Longman Knockouts (1984)
The Methuen Book of Strange Tales and *The Methuen Book of Sinister Stories*, Ed. Jean Russell, Methuen (1982)

The Goat and the Stars

H. E. Bates was born in 1905. He worked as a clerk and as a reporter on a local newspaper before joining the R.A.F. at the start of the Second World War. From 1942 to 1945 he was posted overseas and drew on his wartime experiences to write several volumes of stories about life in the forces.

He was one of the greatest and most prolific writers of short stories and produced over six hundred in his lifetime. 'The Goat and the Stars' is taken from *Short Stories Since 1930 from the British Isles* (Grafton Books) and is typical of his work in its warmth, its shrewd observation of life and its sensitive portrayal of ordinary people. *Fair Stood the Wind for France* is perhaps his most famous war story and in the trilogy about the Larkin Family (*The Darling Buds of May*, *A Breath of French Air* and *When the Green Woods Laugh*, all published by Penguin) we see H. E. Bates at his best as a writer of comedy.

Related reading:

Maura's Angel, Lynne Reid Banks, Dent (1984)
Crick-Crack Monkey, Merle Hodge, Heinemann Educational (1981)

Désirée's Baby

Kate Chopin wrote at the end of the nineteenth century and at that time her stories were considered by many to be too frank and controversial. In her work she describes with great realism and sensitivity the perceptions and experiences of women. Nearly a century

later her stories are still very relevant. 'Désirée's Baby' is taken from the collection: *'Portraits'* by Kate Chopin (Women's Press).
Related reading:

Lesley's Life, Lesley Davies, Longman Knockouts (1985)
It's My Life, Robert Leeson, Armada Lions (1981)
The Gilt and the Gingerbread and *A Story Half Told*, Anita Leslie, Hutchinson (1983)
The Bluest Eyes, Toni Morrison, Chatto and Windus (1980)
The Love Object, Edna O'Brien, Jonathan Cape (1970)
The Laundry Girls, Bill Owen, Macmillan Dramascripts (1973)
The Collected Dorothy Parker, Gerald Duckworth Ltd (1983)
You Can't Keep a Good Woman Down, Alice Walker, The Women's Press (1985)
Women, ed. Maura Healy, Longman Imprint (1985)

The Landlady

Roald Dahl was born in Wales in 1916 of Norwegian parents and after a public school education at Repton College he joined the R.A.F. where he distinguished himself as a fighter pilot in the Second World War.

Roald Dahl is probably best known for his superbly funny and unusual children's books: *Charlie and the Chocolate Factory, James and the Giant Peach* and *The Witches*. But he has also written nearly fifty short stories for older readers on a wide variety of subjects. 'The Landlady', taken from the collection *Kiss, Kiss* (Penguin) is typical of his style: the quiet, uneventful opening, the gradual build up of suspense and the clever and macabre ending. Dahl's biography of his childhood, *Boy* (published by Jonathan Cape) is well worth reading.
Related reading:

'The Murderer' in *Stories*, Ray Bradbury, Granada (1983)
It's About Time: A Witches Brew of Comedy, Tragedy and Other Ghosts, Margaret Chivers Cooper, William Kimber Press (1980)
Someone Like You, Roald Dahl, Penguin (1970)
Collected Stories, Graham Greene, The Bodley Head (1972)
Dead of Night, Stories of the Macabre, edited by Peter Haining, William Kimber Press (1981)
Eleven, Patricia Highsmith, William Heinemann (1970)
Best of Saki, edited by Graham Greene, Picador (1971)
The Devil on the Road and *The Scarecrows*, Robert Westall, Puffin (1981 and 1983)

Vendetta

Guy de Maupassant died in Paris nearly a century ago but his many short stories still make compelling reading. Very often he wrote about the pretentions and snobbishness of French nineteenth century society but in 'Vendetta' we have a powerful story which builds up in tension to the inevitable and horrific climax. The story is taken from *Selected Short Stories of Guy de Maupassant* (Penguin).

Related reading:

The First Forty Nine Stories, Ernest Hemingway, Jonathan Cape (1939)

'The Custodian', Susan Hill, in *That'll be the Day,* Bell & Hyman Short Stories, Bell & Hyman, 1986

The Firstborn, Laurie Lee, Hogarth Press (1978)

A John Wain Selection, Longman Imprint (1977)

The Birthday Present

Marjorie Darke was born in Birmingham in 1929. After training at art college she worked for some time as a textile designer. Her first novel *Ride the Iron Horse* was published in 1973.

Marjorie Darke's stories are immediately enjoyable. She writes in an exuberant style with sympathy, understanding and humour. 'The Birthday Present' is taken from *The Methuen Book of Strange Tales*. The companion volume *Sinister Stories* includes another of Marjorie Darke's stories — *Remember, Remember, the fourth of November* about a superguy who hates November 5th. Her novels, which include *A Long Way to Go* and *Kipper's Turn* (Kestrel Books), show the same lively style and engaging sense of humour.

Related reading:

The Supernatural, edited by Adams and Jones, Anchor Books (1979)

My Uncle Silas, H. E. Bates, Oxford University Press (1984)

Haunted Houses, Aidan Chambers, Piccolo (1971)

Skulker Wheat, John Griffin, Heinemann New Windmill Series (1979)

Summer's End, Archie Hill, Wheaton (1977)

The Third Class Genie, Robert Leeson, Armada (1975)

Thunder and Lightnings, Jan Mark, Puffin (1978)

First Choice, edited by Michael Marland, Longman (1971)

The Ransom of Red Chief

O. Henry (William Sydney Porter) was born in the United States in 1867, and he died aged 43 just as he was achieving success with his writing. Although he never completed a novel he produced some 270 short stories. His stories are immensely entertaining and rank him amongst the very best writers of short stories. 'The Ransom of Red Chief' is taken from the collection *Whirligigs*, which is well worth reading. Also recommended is his other collection *Hundred More Stories*, published by Hutchinson.

Related reading:

Never Wear Your Wellies in the House, collected by Tom Baker, Sparrow Books (1982) [poems]
Joby, Stan Barstow, Heinemann New Windmill Series (1971)
Something to Think About, edited by Paddy Bechley, B.B.C. Publications (1985)
I Want to Get Out, edited by Aidan Chambers, Macmillan Topliners (1974)
The Goalkeeper's Revenge, Bill Naughton, Penguin (1970)
Frankenstein's Aunt, Allan Rune Pettersson, Hodder & Stoughton (1982)

Salt on a Snake's Tail

This story is taken from the collection *Come to Mecca* (Armada) and like much of **Farrukh Dhondy's** writing is concerned with the British Asian community. His stories are powerful, often moving and provocative accounts drawn from his own experience. He has also written *East End at Your Feet* and *Poona Company* (Fontana Lions).

Related reading:

Short Stories from India, Pakistan and Bangladesh, edited by Ranjana Ash, Harrap (1980)
Black Like Me, John Griffin, Panther (1969)
The Colour of a Heart, edited by Roy Blatchford, Longman Imprint (1986)
Walkabout, James Vance Marshall, Puffin (1980)
My Mate Shofiq, Jan Needle, Fontana Lions (1979)
Best West Indian Stories, Kenneth Ramchand, Nelson (1982)
Sumitra's Story and *Rainbows of the Gutter*, Rukshana Smith, Bodley Head (1982 and 1985)
Black Boy, Richard Wright, Longman Imprint (1970)

The Vacancy

Robert Westall was born in Tynemouth, Northumberland in 1929. He studied Fine Art at Durham University and at The Slade School, London where he qualified as a teacher. He has written many fast-moving and highly original novels, the most famous of which is perhaps *The Machine Gunners*, a realistic and powerful story set in the last war. His other novels, which include *Fathom Five, The Watch Tower, The Wind Eye* and *Break of Dark*, published by Puffin, all make compulsive reading. 'The Vacancy' is taken from the collection *The Haunting of Chas McGill*.

Related reading:

Stories, Ray Bradbury, Granada (1983)
The Guardians and *The Lotus Caves*, John Christopher, Heinemann New Windmill Series (1973 and 1975)
Science Fiction, edited by James Gibson, John Murray (1978)
Thirteen Science Fiction Stories, Paul Groves and Nigel Grimshaw, Edward Arnold (1979)
Galactic Warlord, Douglas Hill, Piccolo (1982)
Playing Beatie Bow, Ruth Park, Puffin (1982)

The Most Dangerous Game

'The Most Dangerous Game' is typical of this fine short story writer; splendid plotting, crisp dialogue, full of suspense and graphic detail, a story which keeps the reader guessing until the gripping climax at the end. **Richard Connell** was an American writer famous for his thrillers and two of his stories well worth reading are 'The Sin of Monsieur Petipan' and 'Apes and Angels'. 'The Most Dangerous Game' is taken from the collection *The Looking Glass Book of Stories*.

Related reading:

Desperate Voyage, John Caldwell, Heinemann New Windmill Series (1984)
Ghost in the Water, Edward Chitham, Puffin (1982)
Some Things Strange and Sinister, edited by Joan Kahn, Bodley Head (1973)
Run for Your Life, David Line, Heinemann New Windmill (1975)
Horror Stories, chosen by Bryan Newton, Ward Lock (1980)
The Cay, Theodore Taylor, Heinemann New Windmill (1973)
Chill Company, Mary Williams, Corgi (1976)

Acknowledgements

The editor and publishers wish to thank the following for permission to reprint the short stories:

Jonathan Clowes Ltd, London, on behalf of Doris Lessing for 'No Witchcraft for Sale' by Doris Lessing from the collection *This was the Old Chief's Country,* Michael Joseph. © Doris Lessing 1951

The Mike Haywood Trust, Rotherham for 'The Rose Garden' by Mike Haywood from *Mike Haywood: Some Poems, Plays, Stories and Sketches,* edited by Ted Hartley, Rotherham M.B.C., 1975

Douglas Rae Ltd for 'The Pond' by Nigel Kneale, from *The Gruesome Book,* edited by Ramsey Campbell, Pan, 1980

Grafton Books (A Division of the Collins Publishing Group) for 'The Goat and the Stars' by H. E. Bates from *Short Stories since 1930,* edited by John I. Morris, Hart Davis, 1965

Murray Pollinger for 'The Landlady' by Roald Dahl from *Kiss Kiss,* Michael Joseph Ltd and Penguin Books Ltd, 1960 and 1969

Methuen Children's Books Ltd for 'The Birthday Present' by Marjorie Darke, originally published in *The Methuen Book of Strange Tales,* edited by Jean Russell, Methuen, 1980

Personal essay © Marjorie Darke, 1986

Collins Publishers Ltd for 'Salt on a Snake's Tail' by Farrukh Dhondy from *Come to Mecca and other Stories,* Collins, 1978

Personal essay © Farrukh Dhondy, 1986

Macmillan Publishers Ltd, London and Basingstoke for 'The Vacancy' by Robert Westall from *The Haunting of Chas McGill,* Macmillan, 1981

Personal essay © Robert Westall, 1986

David Higham Associates Ltd for the poem 'Ballad of the Landlord' by Langston Hughes from *Speaking Voice Poems,* edited by Michael Rosen and David Jackson, Macmillan, 1984

Bogle-L'Ouverture Publications Ltd for the poem 'Immigrants' by Sam Greenlee from *Speaking Voice Poems,* edited by Michael Rosen and David Jackson, Macmillan, 1984